# EXPERIMENT
# ONE
MURDER IN THE LAB

# EXPERIMENT
# ONE
## MURDER IN THE LAB

ANNE MORIN

# EXPERIMENT ONE: MURDER IN THE LAB

iUniverse books may be ordered through booksellers or by contacting:

iUniverse
1663 Liberty Drive
Bloomington, IN 47403
www.iuniverse.com
1-800-Authors (1-800-288-4677)

ISBN: 978-1-4917-8498-3 (sc)
ISBN: 978-1-4917-8499-0 (e)

Library of Congress Control Number: 2016900398

Print information available on the last page.

iUniverse rev. date: 03/11/2016

I dedicate my first work of fiction to my very good friends, Dr. Elizabeth Keller and Ms. Eva Csiszar, both of whom are women of unfailing wisdom, grace and constant friendship.

# ACKNOWLEDGEMENT

**I WOULD LIKE TO THANK** Mary Pulsifer, Richard Paulson and Ann Braswell for their editorial assistance; the Ladies of the Lake for their interest and support and my husband Barry Allen for his constant support and encouragement.

## "Experiment"

a noun which describes "a course of action tentatively adopted without being sure of the eventual outcome"

The Oxford English Dictionary

Example:

*"Will murder make the goal achievable?"*

# CHAPTER ONE
## A MOST DEAD LAB SPECIMEN

**YVETTE BILODEAU PARKED IN THE** faculty lot next to the Neuroscience building on the sprawling oak tree dotted campus. As she exited her car, she could feel the breeze snap her curly brown hair across her face. It wasn't the cool wisp felt on a summer's night, but the sharp edge of just enough coldness to predict Fall around the corner. A confirmed academic, the season of Fall for her, was always a time of renewal. Leaves abandoning the trees, shorter and more brisk days usually meant the start of a new academic year filled with new books, new paper, new pens and new students. Fall also meant a resurrection of cashmere sweaters and the wearing of light woolen scarves, more for accessory than for need. Fires in the fireplace and a ritualized preparation of mulled cider seemed so appropriate.

She avoided the sidewalk, choosing instead to cross over a sea of brilliant red, rust and burnt brown covering the lawn. Hearing the leather soles of her loafers flatten the crinkled dead leaves wasn't quite as much fun as she remembered of jumping into piles of them as a child, but it had the same overall effect. The fragrant and subtle smells of flowers in bloom were lost and replaced with the smell of leaves being reduced to smoke. Yes, Fall had its own caché. This morning, however, she kicked the dried leaves with extra enthusiasm, wishing they were the asses of her irritating faculty colleagues. Over and over in a repeating cycle she asked herself the same question. *"With a bajillion square feet of space in a new five story science building, how can they waste precious faculty meeting time arguing over who gets what, how much of it will be for them to own and where exactly will their space be? For heaven's sake, couldn't this be done at another time. Why waste time when time together was the most precious quantity they had and they had so little of it."* On the previous afternoon, she had abruptly left her office after the faculty meeting from hell, packed her briefcase and went home in disgust. Now she had to make up lost time by coming in on Saturday morning.

She knew that the laboratory would be empty today. Talk on the previous morning had centered on the coveted tickets her students had garnered for a homecoming football game that afternoon. Her encouragement of them to all have a good time together had been taken as tacit approval of their absence from their usual Saturdays at work. Now she could try to relax, to be entirely herself and to really get some work done without interruptions.

She reached the large unlocked door to the main corridor of the old gothic styled building and entered the hallowed space. Yvette's tempo changed as she walked down the corridor. While she was looking forward to the solitude of an empty lab, she wasn't crazy about coming in on Saturdays, but she had to complete what she had not finished yesterday. The only thing that had gotten finished after she reached home, were exactly two glasses of merlot.

At this stage in her career, Saturday's were supposed to be her day away from the University and the lab, a day for errands, for herself and whatever she felt like doing that was fun. It was a rare thing for her now to feel pressured to work seven days a week. Occasionally she dropped in to see if her students, who proclaimed to always be in the lab, were in fact, really there. She was even sometimes pleasantly surprised to see them working or just hanging around on weekend afternoons. It reminded her of her own graduate school days when the lab was all that was in her life. Saturday or Sunday and evenings, she could always be found in the lab. Things were different now. Students were so much more casual. She didn't really blame them. Why hurry up to get your degree when job positions were so scarce anyhow?

Yvette's lab was at the end of the long corridor on the first floor of the Neuroscience building, one of the oldest buildings on campus. She was always conscious of the sound of her feet on the old golden oak floor, woodwork worn to a smooth satin finish by untold numbers of scholars and not so scholarly before her. Yvette shuffled with her keys and took out the bright red nail-polish covered one and placed it into the lock of the door. The room wasn't illuminated but she wasn't really surprised. She flipped the switch for a single set of lights which brightened her path along the left side of the three rows of lab benches and back to where her office was. The lab itself wasn't as large as the spaces of her older more senior colleagues but it was significantly larger than the closet she was given when she first arrived at the University.

Time and tenure had helped relocate her into a moderate sized series of rooms. She was comfortable and there was enough room for her students to spread out and not be in each other's way. She was content.

Yvette placed her briefcase on her desk, took out the lab notebook and looked at the clock on the wall. It was 8:20am and time for a cup of coffee. Her office had an empty bench space which supported a small refrigerator and a coffee pot. She liked the idea that she could have a coffee pot going all day long. She had a small sink behind her desk and used it often. She filled the coffee maker and ground up some beans in a little grinder. Fresh grind of rather intense coffee beans was a small indulgence she allowed herself. More importantly, fresh coffee and real cream allowed her to skip lunch. The air filled with a fragrant smell of hazelnut brew and Yvette filled her cup. She settled down at her desk and turned on the computer. She was going to spend some time on the results of her students lab work over the past week.

Yvette was enjoying the absence of laughter, talking and lab equipment sounds. She was sipping her coffee and looking up and out the tall windows. The oak trees protected the lab from the glare of the sun but their longevity on the University grounds had given them time to grow into mammoths whose size obliterated the view and light. The leaves were golden and moving with the wind. Yvette's eyes returned from the oak branches outside the window and something odd caught her eye. Something very odd indeed. She kept her eyes focused on the floor at the end of the lab bench nearest the windows. She slowly and deliberately put her coffee cup down and raised herself up from her seat. Why couldn't she make sense of what she was seeing? Her eyes were focusing on something which her brain wasn't handling very well. Fingers connected to an open palm and the contour of an arm lying on the floor, disappeared from her sight behind the bench. *Could a student have fallen asleep in the lab? Why would they be sleeping on the floor?* She approached the bench and felt her heartbeat picking up. Her eyes moved up the arm and around the corner of the bench. The floor, blackened with the deep crimson of blood, was a stark bed upon which lay the expressionless and open-eyed face of her student, Mike DesFleur. A pungent metallic smell filled her nostrils. Part of his blond hair was a deep burgundy mat. She bent slightly over the body and her eyes started a slow scan.

What she saw wasn't a dead body or even Mike DesFleur's dead body. Her first reaction was of the scientist taking in information, bits of information, facts to be entered into a collection on this type of experiment. *Fingers on the right hand curled but not tightly and apparently not broken, the left hand outstretched and open, a mouth closed with a slight tinge of blood in the crease of the lip. Blood had flown from the side and back of the head and onto his clothes that seemed to be intact. He must have been sitting at the lab bench, now the lab stool was on its side on the floor.* She leaned a little closer and focused on his hands and started to reach for one, perhaps to look at the fingernails when she experienced a wave of nausea and embarrassment and finally, terror.

Slowly, she backed away. *What the hell was she thinking! This was not an experiment to be worked on and written up for publication in one of her scientific journals!* Death of brain cells, DNA, tissue repair and growth factors were her forte, not violent and untimely death of the whole human kind. What was she thinking to be standing here indulging her scientific curiosity while this poor student lay dead! *Whoever did this was probably not interested in being a subject in an experiment to understand the criminal mind. Whoever did this was somewhere else, wasn't he?* The terror had now started to impact on her ability to stand. Her legs were feeling rubbery. Warmth was rising in her face and she felt confused.

Yvette's eyes were frozen on the student's blood smeared face when she heard a clicking sound. Was it possible that she wasn't alone in the lab? She quickly glanced around and backed away till she reached the office door. The clicking sound now was more recognizable as the compressor in one of the lab deep freezers. She had no voice with which to scream and there was no point in screaming anyway. There was no one to hear her. There would be no help for Mike. His vacant blue eyes were not speaking of life but of a rather unexpected and abrupt termination of his experiment with living. She silently closed and locked the office door and put the light off. She reached for the phone and was confused as to where she should be calling. This wasn't a disgruntled student making a fuss for the University police to straighten out. She wasn't even sure she should call 911. She rapidly moved her fingers over the numbers on the phone, dialed "O" for the campus operator and screamed

"Please, Oh for the love of God, please get the police over here, now! I have a dead body in my lab."

Waiting and sitting in the darkness, Yvette didn't dare

move. Her eyes were fixated on the arm lying on the floor. Her mind was racing, darting from one awful realization, one awful memory, to another. Anything to keep the panic out for a few more minutes. Her career as a neuroscientist was up to this point, one of daily low-level stress. The challenges she had met were not exactly of the dead body kind. She would have to control her breathing to prevent herself from screaming and increasing her sense of panic. It would have been nice to have someone special to call in the present situation, but she was a widow without romantic prospects and she had liked it that way, at least up to the present. She could have competed with her young students for the attention of the available male faculty members, but she saw nothing but headaches in that. The thought of her colleagues coming to be there with her wasn't all that consoling.

She sat frozen in place, feeling nothing but the up and down of her chest as she tried to take deep breaths. Her mind wandered to the vivid traumas she had previously endured. She had lost her husband to pancreatic cancer and she was healed from the acute sorrow of her loss but memories lingered. She had envisioned herself living in the lab, quiet and content. Now, she had to get control of her anxiety and see this through.

Pulling her eyes away from the arm and looking down into her lap, she started to pass her hands over the front of her sweatshirt. Yvette was dressed in her comfort clothes, her worn jeans, a soft and tired medical school sweatshirt and her very favorite if seldom worn Weejuns. That morning, she had reached into the closet and decided that this would be a good day to put on her hidden treats. The pair of Bass Weejuns had been acquired a lifetime ago when she had been out of college for a few years and had been worn exactly one day before she realized that penny-loafers were obsolete, had been obsolete when she bought them and had been replaced by sandals worn almost as political statements. There was something about the smoothness and the fine craftsmanship of the leather working however, that made her love these shoes. She couldn't totally abandon them just for the sake of fashion, but she also didn't wear them often either. Every once in a while, she would take pleasure in putting them on, with their obligatory pennies in place. They were not all that comforting now.

# CHAPTER TWO
## THE LAB AS CRIME SCENE

**YVETTE'S EYES KEPT MOVING TO** fix on the dead student's hand, waiting for a single finger to move to indicate what a mistake all of this was. Her own fingers were tightly grasping the edge of the desk and she sat immobilized wanting to be invisible and therefore, safe. As the fear of possibly being not quite alone in the lab began to seriously grip her, she heard footsteps coming down the hallway. Voices were approaching the lab and the door opened quietly. Someone called her name.

"Dr. Bilodeau, are you here? It's Officer Stark from the campus police" A big burly uniformed man followed by a much younger officer entered into the lab and approached Yvette who shifted her focus to the officer's face.

"What seems to be the problem?" was hardly out of Officer Stark's mouth before he spotted the body on the floor. "This looks ..." His mouth was moving unspoken words as he picked up his cell phone and placed a call. The younger officer stared with his mouth agape and stooped closer. He was mesmerized by the dead student's body and didn't appear challenged by the older Officer's admonishment,

"Don't touch anything. Not one thing. In fact, move farther away from that kid, will ya!"

Turning to Yvette, he said with a haltered and softer voice,

"Well, let's just keep away from this general area. I just called the city police. This is their kind of thing. Let's not touch anything. Let's just make sure there is no one here besides us, although it does look like he's been dead for a while." Officer Stark stooped down to look at the body.

Yvette started up "I came in about 8:30am. I really didn't look around the lab. I just went into my office and started to work."

Officer Stark interrupted "You won't want to have to repeat everything. Why don't you wait until they get here."

His voice was aimed at her, but his eyes, like the young officer were staring in disbelief at the young unfortunate student. He could not ever remember a body being found at the University, never mind a body with lots of blood pooling around it. This was more than what he wanted to handle and more than he wanted to be held responsible for. His areas of expertise were stolen books, vandalized cars and jump-starting engines. Death was not his area, indeed. The lab was very quiet as the three witnesses to Mike's body nervously waited for the local police.

The arrival of several uniformed officers from the local police department quickly animated the scene as they moved to secure the area. Yvette, who had finally become calm enough to move out of her office, was quickly escorted right back in and asked a few preliminary questions. One of the officers came and informed her that this was a homicide and she would have to wait for the detectives to arrive. Within a half hour, two detectives arrived and were escorted into the lab by one of the campus police officers. The female member of the team started talking with the police officers and the tall senior detective made his way towards Yvette after having been pointed in her direction. Detective Brandell Young had been a detective for 16 years and unlike Office Stark, homicide most certainly was his forte.

Yvette looked into the face of a handsome and casually dressed black man of about 50 years of age. The glint of the gold shield of his detective's badge attached to his belt, caught her eye immediately. A softness around the orbits of his deep brown eyes was contrasted with the tightness of his mouth. She watched as his eyes scanned the room. Clearly, he was a seasoned professional and most probably saw several layers more than anyone else in the room.

While the crime technicians moved effortlessly around the lab, snapping pictures, dusting for prints and documenting the scene, the detective focused on the attractive professor standing before him. He was taking some notes and kept his eyes on her while he made his mental notes. Impressions are important and can taint or confirm a later assessment. She was attractive but would she be attracted to a younger man, like the victim and he would not be surprised if the young man was attracted to her. She was old enough to be the young man's mother or at least older sister, but that really didn't mean anything. She was casually dressed but looked like she had come into the lab in fresh clean clothes. Hair was in place. Her make-up was fresh. Her eyes were transfixed on the area where the dead man lay and her hands were rolled into fists lying in her lap.

"Dr. Bilodeau, I'm Detective Brandell Young. I'd like to ask you a few questions. Let's start from the beginning. What time did you arrive here?"

"Around 8:30 this morning" she said checking her wrist watch.

"And...." He expected her to continue on.

"Well, I really only put on the lights to this part of the lab" she said as she swept her finger from the door to her office door. She took a deep breath and continued on.

"I like sitting in my office in the subdued lighting when there is no one around. It gives me a sense of isolation which allows me to think. Let's see now, I made a cup of coffee, sat down and turned on the computer, looked through a stack of papers ready to be read, looked out the window and then glanced down at the floor where I saw my student. It could not have been more than a half hour before I noticed him. I was stunned and confused and I couldn't understand what I was seeing. It didn't make sense. Then I got up and approached the body. I half expected to see a student sleeping."

Yvette's speech was now coming out faster. She was searching the detective's face for some shared sense of confusion.

"I stood there for a moment and had to reach out to the lab bench for support. I felt myself go weak from all the blood. I mean, I have seen blood, especially in the lab when we're working on animals and tissues but nothing like this. I have never seen a body like that and it is something, isn't it?"

Her eyes were right there focused on the color of deep

red, blood red with red splatter on the front of the lab bench, blood red tiles and blood red hair. It took some effort for her to stay on track.

"I backed up into the office, locked the door, called the campus police, turned off the lights. I was too scared to leave the office. Then I sat in the darkness and waited."

Brandell scanned the office and saw the coffee pot on the counter. He reached over and placed his hand on the side of the glass pot. Hot enough to at least check out that part of her story.

"Who is the young man on the floor?" He asked while observing her.

"Well, his name is Michael DesFleur and he's a relatively new student in the lab." Yvette was now embarrassed that she didn't know him all that well.

He joined us from an adjacent lab around May and he was really only here to finish up a few details and write up his thesis for his Master's Degree. His previous professor had to retire unexpectedly. I sort of adopted him. I really don't know him very well, as least not as well as my other students who have all been here longer. He seemed like a nice quiet kid. Perhaps you need to talk to some of the others in the lab, some of the younger people who would hang with him."

Yvette did not socialize with her students. She made her own observations about their work habits, their mixing in the lab and overheard perhaps more than she wanted as she worked in her office with the door opened. Yvette and the detective spent the next two hours discussing every detail of the morning's events. The whole time they were in her office, she could not keep her eyes away from the body.

This was a bit surreal for her. The detective asked about the student, his relationships with others in the lab and wanted a list of all the people who had access to the lab. Who had ready access to the lab was a topic she could handle but she was starting to feel woefully inadequate in her lack of familiarity with the details of this young man's life. She felt uncomfortable describing her students. Murder wasn't an activity she could imagine involving any of her students. Her guilt about the paucity of information she had about Mike DesFleur was starting to give her a headache. *No, she didn't know where he lived. No, she didn't know if he was involved with anybody in the lab. No, she didn't know what his outside affairs were.* She felt relief that at least she knew what he was doing for work in the lab.

She dreaded the thought that she would have to call her students, tell them what had happened and prepare herself for attention from her colleagues that she neither wanted nor needed. The lab had always been a refuge away from concerns, a place to lose herself in and now it would not be a soothing place at all. No, it would be a long time before she had another soothing moment. She would never be able to look at the lab floor without seeing the iron-red pigment permeated deep into the pores of the tiles, leaving an indelible mark both on the floor and the psyches of all those who walked over them.

The detective confirmed that he wanted to speak in more detail with her about the lab's work as well as the equipment and general appearance. His eyes roamed around the room and were filled with curiosity about how the lab looked without a murder having happened there. Expensive equipment was lining all the walls and sitting on the bench top. He thought this would be perhaps an interesting case. Brandell hadn't been inside a lab like this and this was a chance to become familiar with something new.

His professional experiences had been in the street, with gang shootings, loveless domestic relationships gone to violence rather than divorce, one drug deal after another ending up in the crapper with plenty of dead bodies to stare at. As the woman just said it was really "something." The lab with all its stuff was sort of fascinating. There was a lot of money invested here. Everything looked shiny and new and clean. Was there something here to kill for?

"Would you mind moving into the lab area itself, Dr. Bilodeau?" It was presented as a question but Brandell having already moved out of the office and into the lab left no doubt that he expected her to follow. His eyes slowly panned around the lab.

"I want you to look around the lab and tell me if there is anything here that you would say is unusual." He took a step back and let her move a bit closer to the aisle. A photographer moved effortlessly around the space taking it all in. While she slowly moved down the first bank of lab benches, Brandell made a mental note of all the equipment which was so neatly placed on bench tops, counters and in every nook and cranny of the space. A place for everything and everything in its place, he thought. He didn't have a clue what they were used for and for this he would have to rely on Dr. Bilodeau to explain all. Most of the equipment was too large to be hefted overhead to clobber someone with. He was searching for something a bit smaller.

"What is this?" he asked as he pointed to a water bath

on the bench top. The metal rectangular box had water in it and a thermometer resting against the inside wall. There was a small red light on the front panel.

"Oh, that's a covered rocking incubator, to keep microfuge tubes incubated at a specific temperature during our DNA cutting." Looking at Brandell's face, Yvette rethought her answer immediately.

"It's a really simple stainless steel bath that we fill with distilled water. We heat it up to whatever temperature we need. With the cover on, we can then set it up to keep that temperature for a long time. Some of the work we do requires a constant temperature and sometimes we even need to mix what is in the tubes while it is incubating so we can make the water bath move back and forth."

"That's something odd" she said as her eyes focused on the red light. "It shouldn't be left on when there isn't a sample in the bath." She started to reach for the on/off switch when Brandell caught her hand and stopped her.

"Wait a minute, please." He called one of the crime scene investigators over. The young woman had her Crime Scene Team jacket and her gloves on and produced a thermometer immediately. She moved the lid further off the bath and placed the thermometer into the bath. She also noted that the thermometer attached on the side was reading 65° C. She quickly noted her own result and turned to Brandell,

"It's pretty hot. The water level is too low. Obviously, a hot incubator isn't going to last if there is no water in it!"

Yvette was irritated that the students had left the bath on. She noted that the students were pretty good about not leaving equipment on. In fact, usually one of the two lab technicians she had, checked precisely these kinds of things before they left for the evening. The crime scene investigator was getting ready to look for fingerprints on the unit.

Yvette had now turned to the large sink which sat at the end of the attached bank of benches at the front of the lab. Filling the sink was a dense cloud of opaque mist. She waved her hand over it and the surface gas cloud undulated like water.

"Oh all right, now this isn't right unless someone has been in the liquid nitrogen tanks and is using something that needs to be kept really cold. It's just a huge hunk of dry ice. You know, carbon dioxide. This is it in a block. We use it with alcohol and acetone to bring the contents of tubes down to a very low temperature before we put them back into the deep freezer. As soon as you add some water to it, you get this cloudy sea. It will dissipate over time."

"Kathy, will you come over here" Brandell was addressing the crime tech.

"Could you remove that piece of dry ice and let's take a look at the sink itself." Slowly, she put her gloved hands into the sink and moved them around. With every wave of her hand, the dry ice thick fog rose up, furled over the edge of the sink and dissipated. She gently removed the remains of two larger slabs of ice, placed them on the counter top and with waves of her hands chased away some of the cool cloud over the edge of the sink.

"Sir, I think I feel something in the sink which is large and cold...maybe ...yes, metal"

Brandell focus intently and watched as she lifted a solid, silver metal hammer.

"Oh!" Yvette recognized it immediately.

"That's Maxwell's Hammer. We use it to break up the ice or dry ice. It's really a surgical hammer which has enjoyed a useful life here in the lab."

"You remember the Beatle's song about Maxwell and his hammer?" she asked as she sought to clarify its name to the detective.

Brandell watched as the tech put the hammer in an evidence bag. He left his crew examining the lab space. Although not a Beatles fan by any stretch, this little ditty was memorable in his youth when he saw himself as a future crime fighter.

# CHAPTER THREE
## REALITY SETS IN

**RAE'S, A VINTAGE DINER AND** Santa Monica institution, is a mecca for trendy West-siders who want an excuse to eat bacon, hash browns and biscuits and gravy without the guilt. The tall, grey-haired man opening the door to the restaurant, watched Yvette walk through and head on to the single empty booth. It had been a Sunday morning ritual with the three of them, older brother Russ, younger brother Michael and sister-in-law, Yvette. Rae's restaurant with the New York Times. The ritual continued even after Michael's death.

Since the loss of her husband, Yvette and Russ Bilodeau had become close friends. Yvette's agitation and lack of sleep was enough to move their Sunday Morning meeting a full two hours earlier than usual. Sunday morning was a time of conversation with Yvette and it was usually conversation totally unrelated to each of their work. There was no romance to their relationship. That would have been like incest. His brother had been married to Yvette for nineteen years before his untimely death. Yvette saw the familiar in Russ' blue-grey eyes, the turn of the mouth, the tall muscular build. It was a warm reminder of her husband. Both Russ and Michael were very bright and each had a wonderful, sharp sense of humor.

Russ took it upon himself to watch over her. His legal expertise as a business lawyer in the entertainment industry was a far cry from Yvette's science so they usually talked politics and books. This morning was different for sure. She was going to lose something major, maybe her peace of mind at the University, her students, her professional detachment, something was going to give. This wasn't going to go away very quickly.

Russ and Yvette placed their identical orders for biscuits and gravy, poached eggs and bacon. The conversation immediately focused on all the unanswered questions which presented themselves. Yvette started in with impatience.

"Hell, I don't even know Mike DesFleur that well. Who is this kid anyway? He transferred into my lab six months ago. You know, he worked with a colleague who had an adjacent lab before he came to me. His mentor liked him enough but since he was going out on sick leave, he had to place the kid with someone. Lucky me! Mike had some skills in tissue culture so I said he could come in. I mean, it wasn't like he was predicted to get the Nobel Prize or anything special. He was just an ordinary Master's level graduate student! He wanted to work on growth factors, do some molecular biology. He did say he wanted to work on growth factors exactly. He wanted to do something with DNA and then get a job with some biotech firm. I mean he was adamant about that. He was really only there to write up his dissertation. I guess he wanted to be around the students who really were doing that kind of stuff. But other than that, I can't remember a single damn thing about him that would give me pause for thought."

Fernando, their regular waiter, gave them hot coffee and took their order. Yvette stared out the window lost in thought and then abruptly as if coming upon a critical fact about the young man started up again.

"He has a really nice car, an old Jaguar. I think it's an XKE from God knows when, kind of a sexy car. He probably has expensive taste but his clothes didn't show it. Like I said, he wasn't particularly outstanding. The young women students liked him though. You know really liked him." She smiled slightly when she thought of his admirers.

"I must remember to mention to Detective Young, how popular he was with the women students. Do you think it was something to do with that?"

Russ smiled slightly and offered his opinion.

"Well, if he crossed one that had the strength to wield a heavy object over her head, he definitely chose the wrong gal!" The comic relief was welcomed by Yvette.

They finished their breakfasts with a curtailed thumbing through the Times and then walked the four blocks to Yvette's Spanish-style bungalow. When they reached the large Jacaranda tree in the front arbor of the home, Russ offered to spend the afternoon with Yvette but she needed some time to take care of business.

As she closed the front door, she heard the phone ringing loudly. She answered it before the machine kicked in.

"Dr. Yvette, this is Jolie. I'm freaked out by Mike's death but I did want to raise a practical matter. I was wondering if you knew when we were going to get in the lab. I don't have anything that needs attention today, but the cells need to be fed tomorrow."

Of all the blessings that Yvette had in her dealings with students, Jolie Raffles was number one. She wanted to assure this wonderful student that no harm would come to the cells. She assured her. "Well, I'll call the detective who is working on the case and see. Don't go there now, please. There's a guard at the door and that will probably be upsetting to see as well as a waste of your time. Jolie, do you know any of Mike's family or friends. I'd like to call his family and find out about any funeral arrangements. I guess I could ask the police."

She hesitated and then added "I'll ask the detective for the next of kin and call them. I will keep you posted if you'd be so kind as to call the others and pass on the information. I think we should go as a lab to the funeral if it's held around here, don't you think?" Yvette couldn't believe she was asking this question.

Jolie answered in a subdued voice "Thank you for calling us up. I'm sure it was awful to have to say it over and over for each of us. I'll take care of arranging for us to go as a lab.

On another note, I don't think we should worry. I think it's kind of creepy and scary right now because we don't know anything, right? But I don't think any of us is in danger, do you?" her voice trailed off. Yvette felt a wave of nausea sweep over her but managed to comfort the worried student.

"I can't imagine why at this point. But maybe that's why the police have locked the lab. I'm sure they have our safety in mind as well as their police investigation. I'll keep in touch with you and anyone from the lab can call me at my home. It's alright. Take care, Jolie."

Yvette may have lied to her student about her confidence in the police's ability to protect them, but she sure wasn't going to settle for that answer herself. She went to her purse and found the detective's telephone number. She wasn't sure she'd reach him at the number but she sure was going to try.

The phone rang several times and after the familiar voice answered, Yvette didn't mince words.

"Hello, Detective Young." She blurted out in a somewhat rushed voice as though she had just had a major terrifying insight,

"Detective Young" she repeated "This is Yvette Bilodeau. I just spoke to one of my students who was concerned that we might be in some kind of danger. I hadn't thought of it seriously until this very moment, but do you think we are? I mean should I be concerned about this?"

Clearly, the tone and spill of words indicated that whether she should or should not be worried was too late to ask.

"Well, I really don't know what to tell you at this point. It's not like a letter bomb was delivered to the lab and the wrong person opened it. We have just started working up the case and I haven't got any ideas about what happened. I think you should be careful and I think you should tell your students to stay away from the lab for a while, unless of course they are asked to come down."

Yvette was somewhat reassured and somewhat surprised at how Brandell had become open and verbose.

The quiet and commanding detective of the previous day had transformed into a somewhat helpful and reassuring presence. She continued the conversation with her questions about the next of kin. The detective gave her an address and telephone number of the young man's parents. They lived about twenty five miles away.

Yvette thanked him. "You know, if I can be of any help, please don't hesitate to ask me. I'm taking some time off and working in my office at home. I think maybe I would be somewhat more relaxed if I could fool myself into thinking that I was really helping. I guess I need to feel in control. Thanks a lot, take care."

"Oh, Yvette, maybe you could help at that, but it's not on this case. I've got another separate case and need to talk to someone at the University about some testing on DNA. Got any ideas on who would be good? We have our regular lab guys you know, that we talk to, but I needed something a little special, you know?" Brandell was into seeing a problem from many sides and a little extra knowledge from an unusual source wouldn't hurt at all.

"Well, perhaps I can help you. Please let it keep my mind off my own lab."

"Alright, I'll stop by your lab this afternoon around 1:00pm. I have some questions about the lab itself" One click and he was gone.

Yvette was a tiny bit pleased that someone from the police department would actually think she could be of some assistance. She always had this notion of her work being very esoteric and unconnected to the world in which everyone around her lived. This would be interesting she thought, a good distraction from the intrusive thoughts which entered her head since she found her student dead in a bloody heap on the floor. On the other hand, she had to go into the lab and that was disturbing enough. Yvette called Russ,

"I just called the detective in charge of the case. He doesn't think we have anything to worry about just yet and guess what? He asked if I would be of some assistance to him on another case. Something about DNA."

"Well here's your chance to play Sherlock Holmes or perhaps I should say Miss Marple" he alluded to her favorite sleuths.

Yvette said she'd keep him posted. She finished reading the newspaper and then left for the lab. She couldn't think straight. When she arrived at the lab, the detective had already circumvented the yellow crime tape across the door and entered into the restricted area. He was examining one of the lab benches and greeted her

"Good afternoon Dr. Bilodeau."

Yvette felt more comfortable with him calling her by her first name and encouraged him to do so. "Please, call me Yvette. It seems more friendly and less intimidating under the circumstances"

"Well, then please call me 'Brandell'"

Yvette didn't mind calling him "Brandell" but she did see the irony in being on a first name basis with a detective investigating a murder. She was also keenly aware that Brandell Young was very sharp. She had no doubt that he would remember everything he was told. She surveyed him more closely, now that he was sitting in her lab, her home ground. She hadn't noticed before how weird his hair was with thick patches of gray hair standing straight up. It must have been that golfer's hat he had worn the day before when she first saw him. She was more cognizant of their respective ages. She figured Brandell Young had at least ten years on her. Yes, she thought, this guy should know the score.

"How are you this afternoon? Can I get you a cup of coffee? Would that be allowed? I mean to go into my office and do that?"

"Sure, I'll take it with some milk. I used to take it black, then I got into going to this fancy café called 'Café Urban'." He said the words with just a little disgust.

"You know the kind that don't serve coffee with cream or milk. They serve café-au-lait and charge you like they had discovered a new elixir. Well, I started to get into some kind of pricey decaf stuff which comes with steamed milk. I guess I've been spoiled. It tastes pretty good even if it isn't high test. No more black coffee to keep the motor running. Now it's decaf with milk to be in with the in-crowd."

Yvette found the thought of Brandell Young sitting in one of the zillion coffee houses that had recently sprung up sipping decaffeinated mocha-java latte, as comforting in a strange way. She would prefer to think of him as though he were an ordinary man, not a man who was obsessed with murders and death.

"You can have rich black coffee with real cream here, if you like, I won't tell anybody."

The detective had carried into her office, a large stack of papers. Yvette found this sort of paper handling a bit distressing. *Shouldn't they be a little neater if anything was going to be organized and solved.*

"I have some news on the case. It seems Mr. DesFleur

was a bit of a ladies man. We're trying to interview the young ladies in his class to see if he had anything serious going on. We've interviewed three so far and it seems as though they all think he had something serious going on with each of them." A small barely noticeable smile on his face dissolved as he continued on.

"We also got the coroner's report. Mr. DesFleur died from blunt force trauma to his left parietal lobe which resulted in a massive cerebral hemorrhage. We've dusted the lab for finger prints and we'll be taking finger prints from everyone that had access to the lab. I still can't figure out how the killer got into the lab, unless someone let him in. We'll see...these things always come out in the wash."

"I have another problem which I thought, since you said you would help out, I'd kind of take advantage, you know. I've got a number of cases assigned to me and my men. Not all of them are murder. Most of the stuff is pretty serious. This other case I'm working on is pretty serious because it involves a big time company here in town. It seems that Biogene was broken into. Whoever did it made a pretty big mess trying to hide what they actually took. But these guys over there have got inventory systems like you wouldn't believe." Brandell took a look at his own stack of papers and laughingly said,

"Maybe I should let them organize me too! In any case, it seems the bad guys wanted to make it look like they were stealing a lot of stuff, drugs you know, but what they took was very specific. The guys over there figured out that someone had taken something out of the deep coolers, you know those tanks with liquid nitrogen. I guess the level of the liquid was really low way ahead of time and they figured that someone must have had the tank open for a long time. So they checked it out and found that some samples were missing. I guess everybody's a detective these days! So my question is 'how long can these samples stay alive or good?"

"Let me see. The samples probably had plasmids with cDNA in them. Biogene is a big gene cloning company. It would be likely that would be what they had in the tanks. I would say they're probably "ok" for a long time as long as they aren't contaminated. DNA is pretty stable with a little protection." Yvette felt confident that she was correct on this issue. She could probably actually help this guy if it didn't get any tougher than this.

"Liquid nitrogen is odd for those unfamiliar with it. It is kept as a liquid in these big round insulated tanks on wheels in the lab. As soon as you open the vent and lower the nozzle, it pours out like the liquid it is. Any spilling over the side of the receiving vessel just dissipates on the floor, creating a cooling as it does. It evaporates quickly, so you have to keep it fairly secure in its holding tanks." Yvette gave a small and quick smile while thinking *too much information!*

"The samples that were taken contained something special that's for sure. But the company doesn't want to tell us what it is. Just that they were stolen."

"I bet they think it's some kind of industrial espionage!" Yvette allowed herself to get melodramatic for the moment.

"These companies isolate gene products and growth factors and make a lot of money from their work. In fact, some companies have even tried to patent human genes, can you believe it. They'll go on to develop some product and mass market it through their own pharmaceutical firm and rake in the money!"

"So you think that this stuff is still valuable even if it's not in liquid nitrogen?" The detective was clearly interested in her response.

"Sure, but I'll bet whoever took the stuff has it sitting in liquid nitrogen right now. Of course, there are many places that have liquid nitrogen. I'll bet there are dozens of places here at the University Medical School. And we're not the only show in town."

"You've been a big help. You don't mind if I bother you again and to pick your brain again, do you?"

"I don't mind at all. In fact, I'll be sure to have some double espresso on hand for your next visit." Yvette was smiling but thinking she liked this guy. It was probably a professional courtesy, but she was acknowledging that he was very bright, bright enough to teach her students a thing or two.

Brandell then stood up. "Well, let's get started in the lab. I want to know what everything does and where everyone sits and I want to know what is on the bench tops, too."

# CHAPTER FOUR
## DIDN'T ANYBODY KNOW THIS GUY?

**ON MONDAY, YVETTE HAD RECEIVED** enough phone calls from the students in the lab as well as the other lab personnel to invite them all over for a meeting. For the most part, Yvette liked the students who were in the lab. They usually worked hard. Her Chinese post-doctoral fellow, Lili Hong was intense, hardworking, and possessed a wry sense of humor. She also wore her ebony hair in a most untraditional short cut with the ends dyed a striking fuchsia. Yvette was always entertained with the way students found to express themselves. If fuchsia hair meant she was now in America and could do what she wanted, well then fuchsia it would be. Lili was also very helpful with the training of the other students. They relied on her and respected her. She was a real asset to the lab.

Jolie Raffles was a stunningly beautiful and delightful Creole doctoral graduate student from New Orleans. She had been in the lab for two years and was making good progress in her research project. Yvette counted on these two students to keep the lab orderly. On the other hand, Rich Kelly was leaving in a few months with the completion of his Master's degree. She was glad to see him go. The personal connections between student and mentor had never gelled. He only needed to have his Master's thesis turned in, defended and then he was on his way.

Her last graduate student, Mike DesFleur had landed in her lab only six months earlier. His mentor had taken ill, left for an extended period and Mike needed a place to finish writing his dissertation. Yvette agreed to give him a desk in her lab. The remaining students were undergraduates, Eric Sanders, a biology major and Sheronice Swain with her eye on medical school somewhere down the line. The last student was Maria Sanchez, a work study student. They hung around in the hope that once in graduate school they would have a place in her lab. The students were industrious and had the kind of youthful enthusiasm that is both inspiring and exhausting to watch.

They had almost all arrived on time, respectful of the notion that they had been invited to their professor's home. This wasn't a usual thing and Yvette had fixed dinner for them. The evening being quite mild, they would eat out on the patio surrounded by deep red and purple bougainvillea and rose bushes. The most senior members of her research group arrived early. Lili and Jolie showed up with cheese and rye crackers, their effort to lessen the burden they felt their mentor carried. Eric Sanders, Sheronice Swain and Maria Sanchez arrived at the door at the same time. Only Rich Kelley was missing.

"But Dr. Yvette" objected Lili "I have very important work. I must get into the lab."

"Lili, everyone's work is important" Yvette reassured,

"but a murder was committed in the lab. This is the most serious thing. A life was taken. It wasn't a lab accident. It was murder and we're involved whether we want to be or not. Now, I have some issues that I want to discuss. May I have your complete attention."

She was being redundant but they all sat in serious silence looking to her for answers to whatever questions were in their heads.

"First, I don't know when the lab will be open as yet. I have been told 'soon', but who knows what that means. I am thinking it means days or maybe even weeks. I am trying to negotiate getting back your lab notebooks. We'll see how the detective deals with that. In the meantime, I want to know if anyone has been contacted by the press."

Eric Sanders, the undergraduate student, had the floor. "Well, I was on campus near the Science complex and there were a lot of reporters. Man...they were everywhere! They were stopping just about everyone and asking if they knew Mike. It was pretty weird. I didn't want to talk to them but another student pointed me out as being in your lab, so they were all over me. I just said 'no comment! no comment!' like I was some government crook being arraigned. I ran over to the library and hid out in the stacks."

Yvette gave a slight smile and complimented him on his course of action.

"I don't think it is going to help if we talk to the press. I wouldn't want anyone to bother any one of you." Just refer them to the police department, she urged.

"Has anyone else been harassed or questioned? ...perhaps by other students?"

"Of course, Dr. Bilodeau. All the other graduate

students are in shock. Especially the ones from Dr. Parker's lab. They knew Mike for three years. I didn't know he had been around for that long." Sheronice rejoined.

"They have all been interviewed by the police and say it was pretty scary. I don't think any one of them had ever been inside a police station, let alone been interviewed." Jolie was very animated as she retold the experience of one of Dr. Parker's foreign post-doctoral fellows.

"One of the Chinese students had only been in the lab for 2 months. If you think science is hard to explain to someone who doesn't speak English, try explaining that they have to be interviewed by the police. I guess police don't have a very good reputation in China. She was terrified. You know the girl I mean, don't you, Mai Ling is her name." The thought of her being questioned by the police made Yvette wince.

However, Lili was a different story. Her command of English improved tremendously since she arrived from China and she shared her experience with the group of her first attempt at dealing with American bureaucracy, the process of getting her driver's license. In the hushed gentle voice the students had come to expect from the Chinese students, Lili summed up her experience.

"It was very bad time. Police tried to make joke about how easy for me to pass because we driving a Toyota. He was, how you say?....a jerk! I am Chinese not Japanese."

"Dr. B, are we going to be interviewed as well?" a nervous Maria brought the subject material back home.

"Of course you are. We all will be interviewed in great depth I should think. I am surprised that they didn't start with us in the first place. But I'm not a police officer so... I don't know their *modus operandi*."

Yvette hesitated and felt self-conscious in her use of police jargon. "I want to urge you to think very hard of anything which could be relevant. Even the smallest detail could be significant. I know this all sounds so melodramatic but did any of us think that we would have to deal with this sort of thing? It sort of makes everything else seem small and a bit intimidating. I know you're all adults but I also want you to know that I am here for each and every one of you."

The conversation in the group turned towards the general lab maintenance while the rooms were inaccessible.

"I am really concerned about the liquid nitrogen tanks, and feeding the cells and monitoring the freezers. What if there's a power outage?" It was Jolie's responsibility to supervise the undergraduate work students. They both worked together to keep the lab stocked and supplied with everything the students needed for their work. It was no small task. The thought of a meltdown or running out of nitrogen sent chills down everyone's spine. It could mean a major loss in DNA given to them from other labs and their precious growth factors so painstakingly isolated over a period of months from thousands of rat, cow and human brains. It was time to be very practical.

"Hold on, I am going to call the detective right now and ask him about limited access to the lab. Perhaps his men could be right there to make sure you didn't do whatever they are afraid you might do!" Yvette grabbed the phone and in a minute was explaining the meeting in her home and the serious and practical questions her students had.

"Well, I can see that this is a problem, but I think that we can help you out somewhat. Why don't you have the students who are going to do whatever it is they have to do, meet me in the lab in the morning, say 9:00am? Is that okay?"

Brandell Young was certainly feeling cooperative.

"I think that settles that issue for the moment. Jolie, I think that means you will come tomorrow. I will meet you there at 9:00am and don't be late. This guy is busy. You do have a key to get into the lab, don't you?"

"Oh, yes I have a key, Dr. B. I had to sign out for it. I only use it when I have to stay late and work with the autoclave. I need to get back into the lab with the clean glassware. Don't worry, I'll keep it safe."

On principle, Yvette didn't feel comfortable with undergraduates having free access to the lab. She had forgotten that she had even given the key to her. The key issue reminded her of Maria's work. She generally collected the dirty glassware in the sinks, washed the flasks and beakers and rinsed them with distilled water. She usually only worked when there was someone else in the lab. The opening of the autoclave could release a tremendous amount of steam and Yvette always wanted someone around in addition to Maria, just in case.

"Didn't Mike have a key to the lab?"

"Of course he did. How else did he ever get in during the late hours of the evening?" Jolie answered.

"Yes, how did he arrange for all those midnight 'tutoring' sessions?" Sheronice said with a slight bit of disgust.

Rich Kelley, one of the quieter and more self-contained

students arrived late and was quickly brought up to date on the issues of police, interviews and Mai Ling's experience with the police interview.

It didn't surprise Yvette that Rich was late. He was a solitary figure, working with his own inner clock ticking away. She admired his intellect but was always uncomfortable around him. She always felt as if she was in the presence of a spider and the lab was his web. He played games constantly trying to trip her up. It wasn't an unusual pursuit of students to test the intellectual command of the Lab Chief. It was almost expected of students to show they could "hold their own". Yvette tried to discourage this behavior by being open about what she knew and what she didn't know. She also made damn certain that if she admitted she wasn't sure of something, she was sure of it the next time she and the student crossed paths. It was one of those little games that are played out in academia. The problem with Rich was that he never knew when the game was over and when to knock it off. Fortunately for Yvette, she had been challenged so many times, she was a pro at deflecting and responding. In her, he had met his match.

Rich was very adamant about getting his notebooks from the lab. He had very important data to review and write up. Yvette had to remind him that a lab mate had just been murdered and that perhaps that took precedence over his own agenda. He took in the information but Yvette wasn't sure it had registered. She knew Rich to be a bit pompous and also that he and Mike weren't close. In fact, they didn't particularly care for each other. That was apparent from lab meetings but at least she expected him to have some grief over Mike's death. She was glad he was finishing up his degree. He would be moving on out of the lab within a few months and then she wouldn't have to deal with him anymore.

The conversation then switched to Mike's personal life. Yvette was out of the loop on this side of the guy and for this she was grateful. Jolie reaffirmed that she didn't think he was making all the moves on his students as was the common gossip. Her views were met with groans and laughter from the rest of the students. Even Lili looked at her and smiled. "Come on, Jolie, how could you think that he wasn't hitting on those young women? The guy made Casanova look like an amateur." So spoke Eric.

He continued on "I swear he was fucking those girls in the lab! Oops, sorry!" as he looked at the flash in Yvette's eye.

"I know that I shouldn't say anything about him now that he's dead but I myself have seen him in the lab with young women when no one else was around. You know... when no one else was going to be around either."

"And why were YOU around, if I may ask?" Jolie was irritated by his bravado.

"Working late as usual Jolie, something which could help your career too if you tried it!' Rich was giving Jolie a jab that she was embarrassed as well as irritated by. She just kept quiet after that. It wasn't that she didn't want to go into the lab at night. It was just that she didn't want to be alone in the lab at night. She wasn't sure what she would have done if she walked in on Mike DesFleur and one of his 'students'. Although she publicly stated she thought Mike wasn't involved with his students, she was saddened by the prospect that he was probably involved serially with every one of the girls coming into the lab and probably every other woman he met as well…except her. Perhaps if he hadn't been so attractive, she wouldn't have had that tiniest of crushes on him. She would have felt more comfortable in his presence. Now that he was gone, she could at least admit to herself that now she was safe from whatever his spell was. She wouldn't be one of his bimbos now!

"I see him work very late some nights. Very late. He even stayed later than me." Lili was now engaged enough to enter into the gossip phase of the conversation.

"Of course, he stayed later than you. He was waiting for one of his mysterious ladies to show up. I wonder what he would have done if she called and said she was coming over and you were still in the lab? He probably would have told you he smelled smoke to send you fleeing out of the lab!" Eric was making the students laugh, although no one laughed for very long. The fact that Mike was dead curtailed their collective sense of humor at his expense.

When the conversation got around to possible motives and suspects, Yvette was totally engaged in the observations of the students. After all she was training them to be scientists, to examine data and draw conclusions, to test their ideas out by experimentation.

Rich raised the issue of Mike's numerous conquests and expressed his belief that rather than some sinister plot, Mike had been the victim of a woman scorned. Yvette found it amusing, irritating and not surprising that he would think that a young woman would consider Mike so great a catch that murder would be the only answer to a rebuff. She wondered about Mike's personal life. In all the time that he had been in the lab, she had never seen him with anyone she would have considered an intimate. Yet, she did have to admit that passion runs high in the game of love. It wasn't like it had never happened before. Murder mysteries are full of the flow of mislaid trust and affection.

The students ran a few more scenarios through as to the possible course of Friday night's events in the lab. None seemed too convincing to her. Her head was full of their speculation by the time they all left her home.

She filled her glass with her favorite Smoking Loon Merlot and sat in the quiet darkness of her living room. Bits and pieces of the evening conversation came in and out of focus.

Mike was liked by the students generally but they had a problem with his seductive behavior. The students could be so self-righteous. If he was fooling around a lot, it didn't seem to interfere with his work. Up till now...maybe. *How was it possible that this guy might have been entertaining the ladies in the lab and she didn't know a damn thing about it. Was she completely out of the loop on this guy?*

# CHAPTER FIVE
## LAB DATA

**ON TUESDAY MORNING, YVETTE RETURNED** to the University. The old stone building spread alongside the parking area was always a source of comfort to Yvette. Its hard wood floors and long corridors were always polished and the walls were covered with paintings and photographs of revered former faculty members and great scientists long dead before the University was established. She always had felt that this place was a refuge for her. More modern buildings were certainly available on campus, but the biological sciences building remained a stone monument and reminder of the commitment of the then new University's reverence for the sciences. She always felt that the biology faculty had gotten the best of both worlds, a wonderful old building with totally modern labs inside. What more could you ask for? She saw two of her students, Jolie and Lili, talking to the police officer who was in the doorway. Yvette approached the officer.

"I was told to meet Detective Young here at 9:00am. The students have a few minimal maintenance duties to carry out to avert a disaster. He was most helpful in letting us come in." Yvette's eyes were searching the young policeman's for some sign of friendly acquiescence.

"Well, I haven't been told anything about that. You'll have to wait until he shows up." The police officer was polite but gave all signs of being unmoving in his stance in front of the door.

"Well, I'm going to wait outside on the lawn. We're a bit early."

Yvette led the students outside where they sat on the small step leading into the south end of the building. There were many students on campus now as classes were in session. Not a few were looking at the building as they walked to classes. Yvette knew they were all trying to grasp the notion of a murder in one of their own buildings. She was thankful that only a few came up to her to ask rather common and unanswerable questions.

"Dr. Bilodeau, why did someone take out this guy?"

"Was he one of your students?"

"This is really creepy! Are they going to keep the building shut for a while?"

Yvette was struck by the banality of the inquiries. "Taking out someone" seemed so "Hollywood" a term for the bludgeoning of Mike DesFleur. 'Taking someone out' in her days as a student meant going out on a date not crushing their skull with a hammer.

Just as the students were beginning to gather in an uncomfortable number, Brandell pulled up in front of the building and parked right there. Not a bad idea thought Yvette as she remembered numerous searches through the parking looking for an empty space. She was lucky most of the time, getting in right next to the building instead of parking at the other end, where the trees were filled with birds and the car hoods with bird poop!

"Well, I hope this isn't going to take long. This is strictly a favor and I need to be right here watching" said the detective as he led the way to the young officer, showed a badge and the door was opened for the entourage. Yvette felt very self-conscious in the lab. It was colder than usual and empty as expected. The students quickly went over the two culture incubators and checked on the gas and water levels. Everything was okay. Lili was moving a large container on rollers across the floor. She placed a long silver hose into the open tank and turned on the liquid nitrogen gas tank handle. She was small and the handle was tight. A firm but determined jerk did the trick and the hose and tank let loose with the usual groaning before the whooshing sound of the liquid nitrogen hissed into the holding tank.

"Oh no!" Lili was upset and looked at Yvette.

"This tank is almost empty. Someone has not kept cover tight. Good thing we come in now or we have big mess. This happen before and I tell everyone to be more careful. We need to order more nitrogen soon."

A sick feeling was beginning in Yvette's stomach.

"Do you mind if I place a phone call into the company? They are pretty good and will be here immediately if I tell them it's an emergency. This is rather critical?"

Brandell gave her the motion with his hand to enter the office and take care of business. She placed the call and came back to the group with a look of relief.

"This is a rather incredible stroke of luck. The company had a truck making a delivery to the chemistry department.

They'll be here in five minutes. Jolie, I want you to stay and handle this."

"Honestly, Dr. Bilodeau, I don't know why we're having a problem with that storage tank. It's almost like someone is leaving the top off on purpose. The second tank is really the more important one though come to think of it. It has the long-term storage vials of all the cells, plasmids and DNA samples. That one seems to be okay." Jolie seemed relieved but annoyed at the prospect of having anything else unpredictable happen.

Yvette grabbed a folder from the top of her desk and started towards the door when the detective asked her what she had .

"I hope you don't mind, but I wasn't supposed to let you take anything from the lab until my men are all through. What you got?"

"Oh! it's just a folder with the minutes of the last faculty meeting and some reports which were handed out. I really don't need them. I guess I have the habit of never leaving the lab without something to read at home."

Yvette was a bit embarrassed and placed the folder on the bench top. The students grabbed their purses and the party left the lab. The whole encounter had taken less than twenty minutes but felt like forever. Once outside the students left for other labs and their other classes. Brandell and Yvette were engaged in conversation for a few minutes outside the building before any students as well as two other faculty members noticed. It didn't take long for the faculty members to figure out that this was a police officer. Who else could get away with parking directly in front of the building! If they were becoming overwhelmed with curiosity enough to approach the pair, they held themselves in check for no one said a thing to them. Yvette dreaded the thought of having to discuss something that she knew very little about.

As the detective drove away and Yvette moved toward her car, she heard her name called.

"Yvette, wait a minute." Calling to her was Tom Hall, a colleague, collaborator and most importantly a friend.

"Are you okay? I mean I can see that you are alright, but I mean are you okay, really okay. I just heard this morning. Kate and I were away for the weekend and I didn't see the newspapers."

Tom Hall was a decent man and a pretty good scientist as well. Students flocked to his classes and he was generally well respected. He was one of Yvette's most trusted faculty friends. He along with his wife, Kate who was in the English department, were two of the few colleagues with whom Yvette socialized.

"Do you have time to have coffee, I don't teach until noon?" Tom asked.

"Well I don't seem pressed to do very much else. I can't get into my lab for a bit now. I am so grateful that I am not teaching this semester. I think I would be in trouble if I had to get access to student's files on the computer. This is very strange and dreadful business here."

Yvette's voice had a note of concern Tom Hall wasn't oblivious to. "Off campus would be preferable, if you don't mind. I can drop you off after. I have my car right here."

The two drove off in Yvette's car to Cleo's Café, the longstanding tradition in the University neighborhood. Long before it was trendy to have cafes with designer label coffee beans, Cleo's café was hosting students and faculty from the nearby campus. The walls were filled with French, Italian and African travel posters, donated over the years by students wanting to leave their mark on the place. Opened in the late sixties, yellowing psychedelic art posters of the Beatles, Janis Joplin and other inhabitants of the decade were stuck here and stayed. These were not reproductions. No, they were the real things left as icons of a past generation. Occasional cryptic messages scrawled on the walls of the rest rooms spoke to famous and infamous people and deeds on campus and helped create its cache.

Community bulletin boards were jammed with "room-mate wanted" cards to notices of lectures on every conceivable topic taking place both on campus and off. It could have been considered a very retro place, a throwback to the sixties except that it was the very same as it had been in the 60's. The 60's may have become the 70's, 80's and 90's but Cleo's was still the 60's and the students loved it.

"Two café lattes, if you please?"

The young waitress took off with the order, stopping at a couple sitting at a nearby table to chitchat.

"Well for God's sake, tell me what the hell is going on!" Tom started in.

"Tom, someone came into the lab on Friday night and bludgeoned a student named Mike DesFleur. I found his body on Saturday morning. The lab is locked and sealed. A detective, Brandell Young, is in charge and now you know as much as I do!" Yvette was glad that this was the first of the faculty to talk to her. At least he had common sense.

"Hmm. Do I know him or should I know him?

"Well, he has only been in my lab for a while less than

six months. He was a transferee. He was hot to do some work on one of the plasmids I was working on. If he had been a better student I probably would have let him work on it, but he was only a 'B'. I think he could have been an 'A' but he was distracted."

"Apparently," mused Tom.

"What did the detectives do in the lab. What do they look for in a lab? I mean we have all this stuff, enough chemicals to destroy modern civilization and paperwork up the kazoo. How do they even know where to look or what to look for? No smoking gun, eh"

Tom's curiosity matched hers and Yvette didn't find the questions intrusive, accusatory or inappropriate. Her thinking was going along the same lines.

"Do you suppose that he was caught doing something?"

Yvette smiled a bit and retorted,

"Well according to my students, Mike was a preoccupied young man alright. Too friendly, with far too many, too pretty girls in the classroom. So say the ladies in the lab."

Yvette continued on. "I think he was an average guy. What do average guys do that makes them murder victims. Stretch a little on this one will you. I think we should be able to make a list of possible scenarios. After all, this is what we do all the time right ...look for the unknown? First of all, he could have been doing something and got caught. He could just have been in the wrong place..."

Tom chimed in "at the wrong time. He could have done something in the past which set him up. I really don't think we're going to have much success on this along these lines. Clearly, he really pissed off somebody."

"But interestingly enough, they think that the murder

weapon was something in the lab. At least that's what the detective concluded. The last anyone said to me was that they hadn't figured it out yet" Yvette's little white lie flowed so naturally from her lips that she didn't even feel self-conscious. It was perhaps not necessary that he know about Maxwell's hammer. She knew that Brandell would not like her to discuss anything at all.

"Not premeditated" eh... is that the lingo that applies?" Tom continued to sip on the hot coffee and look out the window.

"I have no idea when I will be able to get back into the lab. Not that I am in such a big rush, but I do have things to take care of. I hope I will be able to go back into the lab. I have not had this very thought until this moment...."

Yvette was also staring out the window...

"You don't suppose that it was an accident or a mistake do you? I mean, do you think it was Mike they were looking for? What if it was someone else? What if it was me? I can't imagine what would bring someone into the lab looking for trouble. We're only a biology research lab!"

"Yes, but a kick-ass biology research lab! You weren't doing any extra research on the side, you know, "drugs" were you?" Tom was kidding but the little humor it afforded was appreciated as the pair paid the bill and went back on campus.

Tom closed the door to the car and started to move towards the science building, he turned to Yvette and said "Keep me posted! See you at the 4:00pm meeting."

Before Yvette could ask "What meeting?" Tom Hall disappeared into the building. Yvette's curiosity was peaked.

"What's going on now that I don't know about?" she

asked herself. If she didn't know about it, then she didn't have to be there and right now that sounded pretty good. Yvette walked pensively to her car and headed for the comfort of home. As she drove the ordinary route, she tried to empty her head of horror but a feeling of dread overcame her. All she could think about was

"Why Mike DesFleur and will I ever think of the lab the same way again?"

By the time she pulled into the driveway, she had a mild headache and decided to put it all aside for a few hours at least.

"Let the detective figure it out and he can let us know when the coast is clear. I'm only a research scientist, not a crime sleuth."

Yvette came into the house and decided she could relax and read a bit of non-science material. Agatha Christie somehow seemed appropriate. She made a cup of tea, found a quilt and placed herself down in her oversized chair and spent the rest of the day, exploring the details of crimes which could certainly be solved by a simple read of the book and certainly before the real one in her life. Concentrating was a bit difficult at first, but gradually, she engaged in the story, read two chapters and as the knot in her stomach went away, she fell asleep.

# CHAPTER SIX
## SAME OLD SAME OLD

**THE NEXT MORNING, YVETTE WAS** agitated enough at home that she couldn't stay there. She realized that if she couldn't go into her office where would she go? Going to the office was her habit. She would have to wait this out in some other space in the building. When she first arrived at the University, she was given a small room attached to that of a senior full professor on the verge of retiring. She expected that when he left, she could move into all of his space. That was a self-delusion that only spoke to the naivety of a young woman assistant professor. When old Charlie Sloan retired, it was a matter of days before she was informed that the space was to be used to recruit a new faculty and she wasn't going to be able to expand. She was surprised when the "new faculty" was a man, much younger than herself, of no particular importance whose casual arrival caused little stir except within herself. It would not be the first time that she would become invisible to the power figures in the department. In her early years, she questioned the logic of such decisions but quickly learnt that to pursue any kind of injustice which she was the only one who recognized, was a waste of her energy. In time, as her competitors retired or moved away, rivalry for space in the older building diminished and she eventually had moved into the present space. Yes, her lab space was definitely better than a closet but it wasn't available now. It may be that it would never be available again, in the same way.

She would approach the Chairman and make a request. She arrived a bit later than usual and arriving late was a big disadvantage. She would now have to park at the distant end of the tree-shaded lot. She didn't mind the extended lot but she did find the lot rather creepy during the winter months when it grew dark so early. Ordinarily, she would put such a silly fear somewhere in the back recesses of her mind. She would tell herself that a mugging in the faculty parking lot, although probably a good idea from the student's viewpoint, was highly unlikely. Today, however, was a bit different. She felt vulnerable and uncomfortable.

Yvette crossed the parking lot and ran into Dr. Harper, an older member of the department. "I was shocked to hear about the murder in your lab!"

Dr. Harper wasn't exactly a gem at original conversation. Yvette knew this wasn't an overture of genuine concern nor was it likely that Dr. Harper, or more correctly, thought Yvette, "harpy" of the department, was shocked. Yvette couldn't imagine what would shock Helen Harper considering that she was usually the first one to chew on any bit of disgusting gossip and the first to announce at any faculty meeting what horrible things were happening at the level of the Dean's office. No, it was an invitation for Yvette to perhaps give Dr. Helen Harper some choice tidbit of "inside" information, she would be able to repeat like the little gossip magpie she was.

"Well, it's being investigated by the police. Right now I am worried about the welfare of my students, so I have instructed them to say nothing and I certainly can't say anything. I am sure that you can appreciate that." She realized that this would be translated into her being described as neurotically worried about nothing and why would she think that she was so special that anyone would want to hurt her or her students. Yes, Helen was as predictable as the sun rising and a lot less enlightening.

"Well, I'll see you at the 2:00pm meeting."

Yvette couldn't remember what meeting she was talking about. Tom Hall had also mentioned a meeting, a 4:00pm meeting and yet she didn't remember getting a notice. She entered the building and proceeded towards her lab only to be stopped short when she got to the door. A bright yellow police ribbon was placed on the door sealing it off. An officer was inside the lab and he didn't even look up when she knocked on the door. There was no point of trying to get his attention. She put her briefcase down and rummaged through until she found her cell phone. She then removed the detective's card from her purse and placed a call. She was surprised how easy it was to get directly into Brandell's office and even more surprised that he was in. She wanted to know a time line and he didn't have one. But he did tell her an interesting fact,

"Well, we have established the murder weapon. The rather impressive silver hammer that we found in the sink. Blood on it belonged to the victim. Tell me again, what do you use something like that for?"

"We use it to break up the dry ice when we need to freeze some of our samples. We keep it on the shelf at the end of the first counter. It's right there next to the dry ice container, on the right as you enter the lab. You know, dry ice is solid and hard and it evaporates unless you keep it in a cooler."

For some idiotic and subliminal reason, she started humming the Beatle's song. She caught herself and immediately apologized. She didn't want Brandell to think she was callous. She didn't mind if he knew she was nervous.

"You can't use your office just yet. I'm sorry but you are not allowed to touch anything in the lab or office. We're not through with it just yet." Brandell was letting her know that he was firm on this.

She pushed further. "Would you like me to go and look around and give the lab another look-over...to see if anything is out of the ordinary? I mean, I would most likely know right? I don't think I was really with it, on Saturday or Sunday"

"That might not be a bad idea at that. I'll come right over" and with that he hung up the phone.

Yvette got a cup of coffee from the cafeteria and returned in time to meet Brandell who led the way into the now unlocked laboratory. The officer at the door acknowledged his superior and kept his post as they slowly entered the area. With the lights on, Yvette's eyes surveyed the lab. She had given the lab the once over on the morning of their first meeting but she couldn't even remember any details of that inventory. She was too much in shock at the time to be very observant. Now she looked with different eyes, the eyes of a trained observer. Equipment was all in place. She now remembered about their finding the incubator that had been left on. There were no mysterious flasks or bottles of solution that were not supposed to be where they were. She then went to the aisle where the body had been found. The floor had been swabbed but the tiles were still marked with the outline of the dark maroon stain of blood. It would be a long time before anyone would step on that spot, she thought. It would be a very long time before Yvette would ever be able to not imagine the red blood cells seeped into the microscopic crevices and becoming one with the tiles.

Yvette's eyes went to the top of the counter where there were two lab notebooks. The one which was opened was that of the dead student. She looked at Brandell and pointed at the notebook.

"Do you want me to look at this notebook to see what I can see? I mean to say, to see if he was doing something that wasn't quite what we expect? I can do that right now while you wait." Yvette pulled up a lab seat, took the notebook and opened to the most recent entry and worked her way backwards. She slowly read the entries which described the routine assays which the student had been doing. The notebook contained no surprises. Everything was labeled with the normal names of plasmids, enzymes and other reagents in the lab. She was impressed with the neatness of the text as she read and felt that it was a tragedy that this young man wouldn't go on to work in the field. Who knows what he could have contributed. It was a moot point now. She closed the text and looking at Brandell, said

"I don't see anything unusual here."

She looked at the cover of the second notebook and

saw that it belonged to another student, Jolie Raffles. The counter top was where the students left their notebooks, so this wasn't unusual, either.

She got up from the lab bench and walked quietly and slowly around the lab. The microbalance scale was fine, the centrifuge covers were on, no equipment had been left on. Try as she might, she could not see the unusual. She moved closer to the door and her eyes went to the spot where the ice-smashing hammer was usually stored. It wasn't there of course. Her eyes went down to the sink and she saw an insulated ice bucket lying in the sink. Now that wasn't where it should have been but it was hardly important. The students often left the ice buckets in the sink when they emptied them out after working at the bench. No, she could not contribute a single iota of information after this little cruise around the lab.

"I'm sorry that I haven't seen anything at all unusual. It all looks so normal."

Brandell's eyes were fixated on the floor of the lab. "Well, if there is nothing here that's obvious, then there is nothing here on the large scale. The forensics people have been here and have taken prints and examined the area. We'll see what they came up with."

With this, the two of them walked slowly to the lab door, turned off the lights and left the room. "I'll keep you informed and if you hear of anything from students, you will let me know?" Brandell was off to wherever he did his thinking and Yvette was off to an unknown as yet unassigned office space.

On the following Monday Yvette found the lab available. She and the students could start using it again. She was anxious to be in her home away from home. Would it be possible to be comfortable again in that space? Well, time would tell.

She grabbed her briefcase and drove over to the University. She stopped along the way at Cleo's for a hot coffee to go. It was 10:00am, and the place wasn't very busy. Students were in class and it was the quiet time. She was placing her order when she heard her name being called. It was the soft spoken voice of Tom Hall.

"Hey, don't get it to go! Come sit for a moment and fill me in on what is happening." Yvette gave the clerk a pleading look and asked to have her serve the coffee at the table instead.

"I can finally get into the lab. The detective called last night and said it was okay to start using it again. I guess they have gotten as much information as they can from the physical place. I wouldn't know where to start now, if I was in charge."

The young college student brought over the coffee and gave Yvette the curious look which was now starting to become familiar.

"Yes, dear, I am the professor whose student was murdered and no, I did not punish him for not working hard enough!" She was all too aware of the jokes which were now starting to appear among the students. The jokes were always anonymous in their origins but always funny in a sick sort of way. The young student stared at her and said a soft "Sorry, I'm really sorry" and fled the table.

Tom was starting to ask her a litany of questions she now knew by heart. She interrupted him with a diversionary tactic.

"I didn't hear about any meetings and both you and Helen Harper mentioned meetings. I have been pretty good about checking my mail and I don't remember hearing about any meetings." Yvette took a sip of her hot coffee and waited for Tom to speak.

"Well, we had an afternoon meeting on Thursday afternoon. I don't think I am supposed to discuss the reason for the meeting but I will be glad to tell you in another place. This place is too open. Let me just say that it was about a student in your lab. We'll talk in your car after we enjoy our coffee, okay?" Tom took a sip and had no sooner put down his cup than Yvette gulped hers down and said

"Let's go."

The two paid their checks and walked to her car. They sat quietly while Tom described who was at the meeting.

"Well, let's put it this way. You and Howard Lo were the only two missing. Howard is on sabbatical so that isn't surprising. Now, as to the subject of the meeting. Please understand that I really do think that Pete had your best interest at heart." Yvette looked at her dear friend and knew that he too would have only her best interest at heart.

Peter Martin was the Chairman and was generally thought to be benign, respectful as well as decent, a rare combination in academics these days.

"Oh, for heaven's sake! Will you get to the point!" Yvette had enough mystery in her life right now.

Tom started in "There was a report that someone in your lab has committed fraud, stolen other student's work and that worst of all, the work has been published. The Chair received anonymous calls in this regard and was in quite a quandary. He didn't think this was a great time to be calling you up just yet and he wanted some input from the faculty as to how to proceed."

"Alright, alright!" Yvette was staring out the front window of the car, her stomach taking a turn for the worse. She took a deep breath and then turned to him and said

"Names, names please, and what exactly was said." A deep red was coming up her cheeks and now she was mad and really angry.

"Well, it was said that Mike DesFleur had described experiments that were never done...and that he had presented the work at the Neuroscience meeting." Tom was starting to get nervous. He started to speak with a rushed voice.

"I suppose we should tell the detective but do you really think they are related? Do you think that he has to know? It is such a black eye for the University. I can't for the love of me figure out how it could be related...or why someone would place a call now. Maybe it's a crank call."

Yvette quickly jumped in "Why wasn't I included in the meeting and for heaven's sake why wasn't the detective notified immediately? What the hell is the matter with you folks? I want to talk to Pete immediately and I want you to tell me what was said in those calls....You did say 'calls' not 'call' right?"

Tom spoke trying to control his agitation.

"There were two calls. One was a month ago and the second was two days before Mike's death both before anything happened in the lab. Pete got the calls in his office and all the caller said was that Mike DesFleur wasn't working in the lab at night, he was fooling around and what difference did it make anyways, he was making up his data.

The second call just repeated the first and asked what he was going to do about it."

"Well, what exactly DID he do about it?" Yvette asked in disbelief.

"He never approached me on the matter, not once. This is rather serious and could be disastrous for my lab and reputation if it should get out. What the hell was he thinking!"

Tom continued "Well, the entire group just was stunned by his lack of action on this one. He should have at least followed the protocol that the University has set up. Maybe he is overloaded, or maybe he didn't take it seriously."

"Well obviously, he didn't take it seriously otherwise he would have called me in on it. Alright, continue." She urged him to remember every detail of the conversations.

"Well it was a rather short meeting, maybe for a half hour. Peter was duly chagrined at his lack of action. He offered that he had contacted the student's previous mentor but the guy was ill and he didn't want to pressure him. Then he said that he gets these kinds of calls off and on and they usually are empty forms of harassment. Now, he is really embarrassed because the kid is dead! He thinks he should have done something but he doesn't know what exactly."

Yvette took all of this into her head which was starting to hurt.

"He should have contacted me immediately. Why didn't he contact me immediately? I'll never figure you guys out, I swear."

She was furious and it was a sharp reminder of what had been a constant pain in her side since entering the world of academic science. She was continually exasperated by the men in her department, their ignoring her on these kinds of issues and their petty jockeying for power positions. It was this way since she arrived and to the present day and would be that way when she was long gone and dead.

"Well, there isn't a damn thing you can do about it now. We'll call the detective working on the case. He should be duly impressed with the intellectual acumen of the chair's office. I am embarrassed for sure but I can tell you this without a single solitary doubt in my head. Mike DesFleur did not put out anything that I did not check and recheck. I think what we have here is a little snotty revenge on the part of some dismissed bimbo undergraduate girl. Probably she was pissed off because of some imagined or real rebuff."

This was most likely the situation, figured Yvette as she added

"I wouldn't look further than his students, those that he was tutoring. After all most non-science students are probably not that familiar with the process of publishing data or even presenting at scientific meetings. Up, that's where I would start."

"I am going to Pete's office immediately after I check in with my lab. I will ask him about this or "confront" him if that is the right word. He is so damn nice that it will be hard to get too angry but for God's sake, why didn't he tell me? Now this looks very bad. We look like a bunch of uptight jerks and maybe not too bright jerks at that." Yvette was disgusted.

"By the way, what was the other meeting about...the one at 2:00pm that Helen Harper was mentioning?" she asked as she started looking for her keys.

Tom answered with a sense of relief.

"It was a brief meeting of four faculty members to discuss the text to be used for the Fall semester in Bio 101. I know you were on that committee but Pete thought you were too distracted or busy to put some time into it. Basically, we're using the same text as last year. The students will appreciate that as they will be able to sell their texts at the campus store. It was a nothing meeting."

Tom reassured her. "Honestly, it was a 30 minute meeting during which everyone had their say and then we did what we originally planned to do. You didn't miss a thing."

He got out of the car and ambled over to his own car and was on his way back to his office on campus.

Yvette sat in her car feeling nauseated. Was it possible that this kid had screwed with the data? "No way" she told herself. I have checked everything he did. I even checked while he was doing his work. Plus, I have seen the raw data. Plus, he came with a recommendation as to the quality of his work. I am going to check it out with the other students. They always seem to have a different line of communications than the faculty.

# CHAPTER SEVEN
## WHAT ELSE IS GOING ON?

**THE NEXT MORNING, YVETTE MADE** her way to campus, found a single parking spot near the science building and gathered up her briefcase to enter, or more accurately, to reenter the world of science. She passed unnoticed into the building which wasn't particularly empty or busy, being that time of day when students were either in the labs working or in class. She approached her lab and was prepared to see the yellow police tape across the door. It had been removed and now it looked more normal. She had not told the students that they could come just yet. She needed to feel safe before she would let them inside. The lab was or should be a place second only to home and a place where thinking about the science was paramount. It shouldn't be a place of intrigue or life-threatening misadventures and danger.

She put her briefcase on the floor and searched in her purse for the red-coated key. She placed it in the lock and slowly opened the door. She picked up her briefcase and started to enter the quiet darkened lab. Three steps in and she hurled forward, her body slamming the floor, her head barely missing the edge of the sink counter. Her purse had flown out of her hand and was lying in front of her while her briefcase was laying at her side with some of its contents spilling out. Her face pressed against the cold tile for just a quick moment before she lifted it up. She was stunned but not so shocked that she didn't feel the presence of another person in the lab. A rush of cool air moved over her sprawled legs. What seemed like a springing bodily movement exiting the doorway, wasn't a figment of her imagination. She stayed frozen on the floor for a moment longer then quickly got up and rushed to the door. Flinging it open she looked into the corridor. The freshman biology class was just over and the corridor was filled with students. How could she possibly know who had been in the lab? She couldn't.

She turned back into the lab, closed the door, looked around and made a mad dash for her office. She locked herself in and called Brandell. He wasn't to be found. Next, she called the campus police. They arrived quickly drawn by the call and the potential drama.

"I didn't imagine it. No, I don't think so." She was shaking her head and looking at the floor. Once said, she had given them an excuse to dismiss the event as a figment of her imagination. The campus officer thought it wasn't the act of an hysterical woman, just the over active response to a simple fall in the lab. After all, he too might hesitate to enter that room again, wouldn't he. "I think we must secure the area and call the detective, just in case" said the officer. *Just in case what* she thought, *just in case of what?*

She assured them that the lab looked really normal.

The lights were off and the lab benches were clean. She called Brandell's office again. The city police assured her that Detective Young would get back to her as soon as possible. She was physically alright, just a little shaken. She didn't really want to stay in the lab or her office more than she needed, at least not today. She would go home and let her blood pressure return to normal. Whatever she had to say or ask of her chairman could wait.

She went home and sat quietly in her study looking at the wall. Then the phone started to ring. It seems every student had called her to see if she was all right. The last call was from the Police department indicating that Detective Young was on his way over to her house and needed to speak with her. She brewed fresh coffee, waited patiently and became aware of a nauseating feeling that maybe it had been just a fall, a reaction to the lab as a crime scene.

The doorbell rang and she found the detective to be dressed more casually than her last encounter with him. Shorts and a sweater...very informal indeed! Yvette offered the detective a cup of coffee, remembering that he liked plain "coffee," not java, not Kona, not latte . . . just plain coffee, as in "just the facts Ma'am..nothing but the facts!"

Brandell gave her a quizzical look and started in. "I got the basics from the campus police about this morning, but I wanted to hear it from you again. I was out on another case when you called and this is the soonest that I could get back to you. Sorry about that."

Yvette now became slightly agitated and for some reason, embarrassed.

"It was midmorning. I entered into the lab and I fell forward on my face. I thought I felt someone pass over my legs and exit the lab but when I got up and checked the corridor, there were too many students to see any one individual. I'm confused about it. Do you think that I could be so mentally agitated that I imagined the 'someone'?"

The detective took a long look and then turned his eyes to the window.

"You've been doing your kind of work for a long time. I think that, barring finding a dead body, your instincts and powers of observation are probably second nature by now. If you think that someone pushed you, then I'd bet that someone pushed you."

Yvette's mind was wandering to her finding the student. She was grateful that she had never shared with Brandell her initial professional fascination with the dead body. Yes, her skills at observation, making mental notes were pretty well honed. However, she was still a bit chagrined that she was capable of being so callous about the body. *But it wasn't really being callous*, her mind was churning. *It WAS a fascinating experience! How many people would find it gripping to be really close to a murdered person, close enough to touch the coldness of the lifeless body? To be alone to observe the dried and spattered blood? To actually see the dented skull with exposed brain, the exposed "self" of the dead person released from its protective vault? To be close to the chest insulted with a mere slip of a bullet? The neat or jagged edges of the soft flesh of a slit throat? Oh, they would put up a fuss, denying their morbid curiosity, but the phrase "morbid curiosity" had easily become part of the language because people DID have morbid curiosity. After all, all those television crime shows were very popular for a reason.*

Brandell brought her attention back by ignoring her seeming distraction and continued on "We have taken fingerprints on the door but there were so many, I'm not sure that we're going to get anything from it. I think that we may have to put a surveillance camera in the lab" She felt a bit relieved. He wasn't dismissing her encounter with a phantom and even better he was going to take some action.

He continued on talking "Right now, I think I need a bit more information from you. I need to know what exactly it is that you do in the lab. What kind of stuff do you have hanging around? Information like that."

Yvette was taken aback by the direction of his questions. He wasn't asking about Mike, but about the lab and her work.

"My lab has a few projects going at the same time. Mainly, it's involved in looking at the activity of growth factors. We're looking at stem cells and how they work in a particular model of spinal cord injury and some of the students have some minor exploratory projects related to these. We're also working on the expression of genes in these cells and do a considerable amount of work with DNA. I have about $400,000 in National Institutes of Health grant monies and some support from the university."

For Yvette, it was a new experience describing her whole professional life in a couple of sentences. It had taken more than twenty years of experience to get to this simple place.

"What are the implications of your work? Um, I mean, is it very competitive? Do you get a lot of money from inventions?"

Yvette smiled as she thought what a good idea it would be to actually get money for some of the practical aspects of her work, but she wasn't a science entrepreneur. In fact, she held those guys in contempt while simultaneously also wishing she could be more like them. It wasn't likely that she would take one of her isolated factors and use it to start a company. She had two colleagues who had done just this same thing. They were now "sitting pretty" as they said in speaking of their efforts. *AcCELLuration* and *Neurogenerex* were the two start up biotech companies which attracted the attention of foreign investors, making her friends independent of academia and more importantly, independently wealthy. The concept of the pursuit of wealth through science was one that escaped her.

She was happiest in the lab and money wasn't a motivating factor. She knew she was naive in this way but it was okay. If she had to swim with sharks, at least it was in a pool that she recognized. On the other hand, if she could learn how to think about science from the business angle maybe she, along with the university, could cash in on her results. She didn't have time for learning about business, she told herself. She had majored in biology and not business for a reason. The explosive money-making in biotech would be another event which would pass her by.

"I want all the details of what you do" he continued.

Yvette took a deep breath and started in.

"We're a very basic research lab. Our goals are to understand what makes the cells of the nervous system make connections and 'grow' which I guess could be interpreted as 'learning' in some circles. I have no money from drug or biotech companies. We use human and mouse cells we isolate from living tissue and then we keep them alive in the lab. This is called culturing the cells and it's expensive and demanding. It's cheaper than using living animals, but even cells need to be fed and kept alive, so it's labor intensive. Lili and Jolie take special care in keeping the cells alive. I have several factors which could be considered 'hot' items. They are, oh what's the best way to describe them...they are 'timely'. One is interesting but seems to need something else to work with it. We're calling it for the time being, 'helper' while another one is really powerful and can really make neurons grow their processes. We call this one 'GAGA' which is short for glial-associated growth agent. Glial cells are sort of baby sitters for neurons which are really the workers of the nervous system."

"GAGA is one compound that could make a major difference. I mean if I were a betting woman, I would put my money on this one. We're getting really good results so far."

Brandell interrupted "So what does it do and who knows you have it?" Yvette laughed.

"Well let's see, everyone who was at the last Neuroscience meeting, that should be about 20,000 people and then...."

She looked at the detective and saw that look she recognized, the look of those not familiar with how the scientific literature worked. There were not a lot of secrets the way most scientists did their work. Now, private companies, well that's a different story. They do business science, which is a horse of a different color. She continued on.

"You see, we have published this work and will continue to publish it as it unfolds in our lab. My colleagues all around the world email me and communicate all the time about this and all of our other work. The federal government, that is, your tax dollars, fund this work. So it has to be there for all to see. If I were working at a drug company, very few people would know what I was doing and even fewer on the outside. There work is their financial future. They are much more profit oriented and much more practical than we are. We both do our thing." Brandell pushed further

"Would anybody want what you're doing? What do these factors do? I mean would anybody steal this kind of information or these things?"

Yvette began to see where he was going with this line of inquiry.

"I haven't given GAGA to anyone because no one has asked for it. In fact, we're doing some work which I haven't yet reported. Everybody sort of has their own factors to work on. We have started to use it on a model of spinal cord injury."

Seeing her chance to enlighten the lay person, albeit a very smart and attentive lay person, she continued.

"What do you think is the major problem with spinal cord injuries? I mean, why do you think they have always been considered so disastrous from the viewpoint of healing?"

Brandell confessed he didn't have the slightest idea why these kinds of injuries were so poorly mended. In fact, he like so many others, took it for granted that a spinal cord injury was one of the worst you could get. He knew of more than one victim of drive-by shootings who got it in the spine. He could see them hanging out in the hood in their wheelchairs.

"There are some pretty interesting events which occur

during and after a spinal crush or injury. The fact is that the body is pretty good at cleaning up a local mess, like a crushed or bruised cord. In fact, it's too good. In the rush of all the special cells to clean up broken cellular parts, blood cells and other debris, they create their own problem. They get in the way of the repair process just by being there. Physically, they are in the way of the nerve fibers which might be able to reconnect, if the way was clear."

She checked to see if he was listening.

"Let me explain it another way. You see, the spinal cord could be compared to a telephone cable. If a storm causes a tree to break service in the telephone line, the repair guys come out and fix it. They just stretch it out and reconnect the whole cable. If the cable were to break in two, now that might be a different problem. That would take longer because they would have to make sure that the wires were connected properly. The repair process would be very complicated if they didn't have some kind of way of knowing how to reconnect the wires so that the Smith household wasn't getting the Jones' phones calls! In the living body, cord injuries of all kinds may have a problem with the cells whose job it is to do clean up. They cause an inflammatory response which can permanently alter the environment so that the 'wires' or processes of the cells in the nervous system cannot be 'hooked up' again."

"Today, they routinely give a treatment to stop the inflammatory process in these kinds of injuries. I mean they give treatment immediately. It is amazing how effective it can be. You see, damage can continue to accumulate even after the primary injury. The idea is to stop it and then help the tissue mend itself through directed reconnection.

That's where the cellular factors come in. They help the important parts of the cells in the cord to repair. This is really new, cutting edge stuff. We do not know all the factors, so everybody is looking. You know how many spinal cord injuries there are every year?....a lot!"

Brandell interrupted "So has anyone ever tried to get you to give over your work to be developed for commercial purposes?"

Yvette gave a quick "No" for an answer. "I don't even know if it will work in humans. It seems to be pretty good in helping mice heal their cords but that doesn't mean that it will work in humans. Plus we have to identify it first before we can make enough to make it available in any quantity. Why are you asking about this? Are you thinking there is some connection to Mike's death?"

"I am trying to understand what has happened in your lab. You didn't fall in the lab, you were pushed. Now assuming that you don't have an enemy, some disgruntled undergraduate pissed off about their grade, we can conclude that you surprised someone in the lab. Why were they in the lab and what the hell were they doing? Okay, let's start from another angle. What kinds of drugs do you have in the lab?"

Yvette ran off a list of the special registered reagents and drugs in her head.

"Anesthetic to put the animals to sleep, should be easy enough to check that since we keep extremely detailed logs of them, plus they are under lock and key. Alcohol to sterilize things. Actually, it's right out on the bench, nobody would break into a lab to steal a bottle of 95% ethanol. It's right there all the time. Okay, let me think...

ether...no, no. We don't have any ether anymore. It's too dangerous, very explosive, you know....I can't think of anything that would be considered 'illicit' or 'recreational'. You know if someone wanted to get into the recreational drugs, they could go into Tom Hall's lab. He's the psycho-pharmacologist or 'drug guru' as we affectionately call him. I can't think of anything that would be high on a list of desirable diversions."

Brandell asked his last question. "What was Mike working on?"

Yvette refilled her coffee cup and offered Brandell a refill. Mike was in the lab a relatively short amount of time but he was interested in GAGA and the second factor, Helper. He was looking at its distribution in the spinal cord...and I believe he was looking at it in the cultured cells as well. He'd not been in the lab for very long. He was really just getting started."

Brandell finished that last of his coffee and arose from his chair. "By the way, I had an interesting conversation with the Chairman of your department. It seems he got two phone calls from a distraught young woman who made some pretty awful claims about DesFleur. She essentially accused him of falsifying data and presenting it at the Neuroscience meeting. He let it rest a few days, trying to think how best to approach the problem when the accused student is then found murdered. Well, the young lady caller showed up at his office within a few hours of the news getting out and she was crying her eyes out. Seems, she wanted a little revenge for being dumped. What better way than to accuse Mike of misconduct. She begged him to forgive her and to forget the whole thing. Of course, he did forgive her, scold her, tell her he had to tell it to the Dean and let him deal with it and then he called me."

Yvette sat flabbergasted. Not even a word to her about the whole thing. "Well what did you do about it?"

Brandell gave a slight smile. "Apparently the girl was at home with her parents in New York City for that weekend so, he just let it go. Can you believe it! Talk about bad timing!"

He started to walk around the room. He wanted to know where did Mike work, who sat and worked at each bench and what each piece of equipment was used for. Yvette felt like it was worth it to actually explain how things went in the lab because Brandell seemed to understand more than the average guy. Right now, the whole thing was a big enigma, but it wasn't likely to be so for long. Murderers usually get caught and murderers in academic halls are probably no exception. In fact, Yvette thought academics might even be worse at evading because they were so damned confident, or arrogant, depending on how you viewed them. There were perhaps enough jerks like that to give legitimacy to the complaint about snooty professors or scientists who thought they were smarter than most everybody else. She could not imagine a colleague committing a murder but then again, this wasn't something she gave a great deal of thought to. Now, if she daydreamed about bumping somebody in the department off, well who hadn't had such thoughts themselves.

The remaining two hours were spent talking about the students in the lab and she was satisfied that she knew enough about them that she could answer every question he asked. By the time he left, he was convinced that she was probably a pretty good scientist, a really good teacher and had sufficient brain power to probably serve as a good source to bounce ideas off. He was reasonably sure she had nothing to do with the murder and was a bit surprised that she wasn't more concerned about the pushing incident. He thought he would have to keep an eye on her if she didn't have any sense outside the lab.

For Yvette, the rest of the week passed uneventfully. Students were back in the lab, the surveillance camera was working and it was a short work week. The Columbus Day holiday was here and she headed for the mountains for a few days retreat and rest.

# CHAPTER EIGHT
## BRANDELL SETS A COURSE

**THANKSGIVING HOLIDAY WEEKEND, THAT LONG** awaited break in the Fall semester came and went. Now the students and faculty prepared for the end of the term. There was still a lot of information to be crammed into heads and a few exams to be meticulously prepared. Yvette was grateful that she wasn't in the classroom this semester although perhaps it would have been better to be distracted by the hours spent in front of students. For Brandell Young, the Thanksgiving holiday was a single day of overeating and gathering with the family. He was senior enough to be able to take the day off.

Brandell was one of the respected uncles in a large boisterous family which celebrated every holiday over food, more good food, and nurturing conversation. His long climb up to the senior level and into the rank of Detective was one which was admired and gave him credibility as a sage. His low *basso profundo* voice gave him a place in the quartet of men who rallied the family in songs, both of the pop variety as well as a number of church choir songs. The music was thread woven into the fabric of the clan, uniting the young with the old and carrying on tradition. The food was the other draw. The large family and all the others who were by friendship and love considered family, required at least two turkeys. Brandell had overeaten by sampling every single dish on the table and now, he was content to sit quietly and think.

He wasn't so much glad to go into the office on Friday as relieved that a few of his detective friends had taken the extra time off for an extended break. Now he could assemble his thoughts in peace. Although he had more than one case in his active file, this current murder at the University was puzzling and difficult. He sat quietly and reviewed his notes taken while interviewing everyone in the lab. What did he have on the victim? Well, he was young, twenty six years old. He was pretty good looking and fascinated with the ladies. He apparently only concentrated partially on his work, spending a notable time dating.

Now the important facts. He was liked by his students even though some of them may have looked down on his philandering. Yes, Brandell could tell that the young women in the lab disapproved. He didn't sense the kind of disapproval that would have required death to make it right however. He wouldn't be surprised if one or two of these young ladies had been the recipient of Mike's attention in the past. That wasn't going to be an angle to pursue at the present moment. Brandell was going to focus his attention on the work which Mike was doing. Perhaps he was involved in selling his work. Brandell could now see with his seasoned cynicism that a young man could probably make money for himself if he were clever enough to stay one step ahead of everyone else. He was going to ask Yvette to review this kid's work.

Brandell pulled the folder over containing the forensics lab results. He opened the page which outlined the fingerprint results. Every print found on the lab bench, door and door knob fit someone who was in the lab. The prints on the hammer were unreadable. That was a shame. He looked up and out the window and made a mental note that this was most likely an unplanned event. Who would carry a silver hammer with them just for the hell of it? On the other hand, who would know that the hammer was ever there in the lab or where it was stored? The time of death was put at around 11:00pm to midnight. This wasn't a particularly weird time for the lab. The presence of lights in the lab would not attract attention. Dr. Bilodeau had already said that students stayed up quite late in the lab. No student admitted to being in the lab that late that night however. The Chinese student, Lili had been there till about 8:30pm, he thought he remembered her saying. The thought of Lili wielding a hammer wasn't one he entertained for very long. Perhaps someone had come into the lab and surprised Mike. Or perhaps someone had made an arrangement to meet him there. That could explain how the killer entered the lab. Brandell started to review his interview notes. Yvette had quite a few students but he wasn't surprised. She seemed not only smart but accessible. Students would gravitate towards someone like that. He started down the list.

Sheronice Swain, he thought, was a pretty young black woman who reminded him of his own daughter. She had a good sense of humor and was confident in herself. He was in a strange way proud of her. It was as though her success was indicative of the success of his own daughter who was away at school and who he did not keep in touch with as much as he should. Sheronice had been out on a date on that Friday evening. "I was out with my fiancé. We went to a movie and then back to my place."

She did get a little tense when Brandell discussed the love life of Mr. DesFleur. With a little prodding and a direct question, he had managed to get out of her a description of her own interest in the young man. "Oh it was so embarrassing, really. I was so stupid and naive, like all the others. I guess I was lonely or something, plus he was so attractive." With this the young woman gave a slight sigh. "I willed myself to not think about him as a human being but rather as a snake. It helped."

Brandell read his notes and was reminded of youthful sincerity and vulnerability. She may have been another flower in the garden of life for Mike DesFleur to pollinate, but Miss Swain was no shrinking violet to weep over lost love. She was in a class of her own. She was now involved with a graduate student from the Law School and in fact, mentioned that they had even spoken of marriage. It didn't seem like she was pining away for the victim at all.

Lili Hong was a fascinating exposure to another culture. She was tiny, dressed in blue jeans and spoke with breathy hushed speed with her dimples showing up. She was fragile in appearance with the interior of a survivor. Brandell enjoyed her interview the most. Her father had been an educator during the Cultural Revolution and had suffered immensely in his life. Her parents had sacrificed to get her out of the country and into a good school in America. She was so proud and he thought, so typically American. She described many hours in the lab and Brandell thought she was probably the typical student. She wasn't enamored of Mike, probably because he did not find this flower to his liking or perhaps she was on to him so quickly. She revealed that she was involved with another Chinese postdoctoral student in the geology department, and he took up whatever free time she had. Brandell could not see any issues she might have with Mike.

The next set of notes included the interview Brandell had conducted with one of the male students in the lab. Eric Sanders was a bit more puzzling than the other students. He was an undergraduate and gave the impression that he was probably getting ready in the next few months to move on to the real world. Brandell was going to keep an eye on him. There was something about him that wasn't quite right. He had been hanging out in the lab for the last two years. He would be graduating in the spring and then gone from the lab. He had a regularly scheduled racquet ball game with Mike and considered him a friend. In fact they had been friends even before Mike transferred into the lab. Eric had encouraged Mike to move to Yvette's lab. He thought that Mike could make more progress working on growth factors if he was in the bigger and he thought, better lab. What was he doing on Friday night? He went out to have dinner with a couple of other students and went home. No one saw him at home as he lived alone. Brandell had watched Eric's eyes the whole time they talked. Eric would look away most awkwardly. Brandell wanted to speak to him again, perhaps with another detective present. That ought to scare him enough to pay attention to the questions and be straight forward. Eric was around the same age as Mike, just as handsome and could have been a competitor for some unlucky female. He definitely wanted to see him again.

Brandell turned the pages of his notes and came across his account of his conversation with Jolie Raffles. Now here was an odd duck, he thought. Jolie Raffles was a pretty southern creole girl of dark and lovely complexion. In fact she was downright beautiful. She spoke with a southern but not quite place able accent. She was charming. She actually made Brandell laugh as she described Mike's behavior, the clothes he wore and his penchant for fast showy cars. She was very observant and even knew about Sheronice's affair although Sheronice had made her swear to never reveal this fact. Jolie laughed hilariously when she commented that if every young female student who had come to Mike for "tutoring" had actually got tutored in biology instead of God-knows-what, they would have ended up with a stellar class of scholars. Mike had tried his piercing good looking eye stare just once at her as she returned his look with a good contemptuous optic scalding.

Brandell looked again at the class line up and saw the name of the last student, Rich Kelley. How did he come across? He was self-possessed, smart, and seemingly straightforward. He did not dislike the victim and had socialized with him outside the class. He once shared a room with Mike at a national meeting of one of their science societies. He had worked in the lab up until 7:00pm the night of the murder but didn't see anything amiss. He left to get coffee at Cleo's. Brandell thought that should be easy enough to verify.

The last person he thought of was the lab chief, herself. She was attractive and very smart. She was definitely shaken up. *Where had she been? That's right... she had been at home. She's old enough to be this kid's mother....no, older sister. She took a tumble but I think she was pushed. It didn't bother her as much as it should have. Well, we'll keep this thought in the back of our heads and wait.*

Brandell made a list of issues for his underlings to pursue.

"Check out where everyone had been," was on the top of the list. Brandell wanted to pursue another approach which would require a bit of intellectual stretching on his part. What was it they did in that lab that would draw attention?

# CHAPTER NINE
## BUSINESS NOT AS USUAL

**RON HATTORI SAT UPRIGHT AND** transfixed at his desk in his office in the high rise office building of Rising Sun Landmark Investments. His eyes were transfixed by the computer screen's changing images. His was a lavish office for a young man his age and he occupied it with both a sense of entitlement and a dash of paranoia. On his solid ebony desk was the lightweight top of the line Dell laptop computer with its flickering screen, a silver block holding a clock, a pad of paper, his nameplate, and a single Mont Blanc pen. His walls were tastefully decorated with his framed University diploma flanked by two matching silk paintings, gifts from his grandmother. On a side wall was an enlarged framed picture of his fraternity brothers. On the other side wall was a picture of himself and two friends in their kayaks. Ron looked moderately self-conscious and not a bit comfortable.

In one corner was a rather impressive six foot high hand-painted silk screen of lotus blossoms while a large vase filled with yellow tulips sat on a nearby glass table.

His clean Asian-inspired decor was less for himself than to impress his Asian clients. He had been expressly hired to attract and court this particular clientele. Ron himself was a moderately handsome young man with no particularly outstanding physical features with the singular exception of his height, which was a firm six foot three inches tall, well over the usual height usually associated with Asian-Americans. Thus, he surprised many a client as he rose to shake their hands. This height was just one of the many gifts he possessed, a symbolic gift destined him for bigger things in the company. Surely the assignment of this office space was a sign of the company's confidence in him. The fact that it had no windows and that he had furnished it himself, did not give him any cause whatsoever to rethink his position with the company. Surely they let him set up his office himself because of their deference to his good taste.

Ron's given name was Maseo Hattori, a name belonging to his grandfather for whom he had been named. "Ron" fit him better he decided when he turned 15 years old and it had been "Ron" ever since. Although Ron could speak fluent Japanese, he was totally a product by birth of every freedom of the United States. Born in the West Los Angeles area, he had moved to the company's main headquarters. He wasn't what he considered "a computer nerd" and he wasn't going to be thought of as a "typical" guy of Asian-American descent who lived, breathed and dreamed about computers. He kept his distance from the company's own computer experts. Ron didn't even date the female computer wizards. No, his interest lay elsewhere.

He had come to work for the firm right after college

and had been there for two years. He entered into the business world with little practical experience but with a distinguished academic record in his business major. Business, the unfettered pursuit of it, the manipulations of people in it, the immense promise of unfettered wealth which flowed from it and the unpunished immorality of executing deals in it, were his life and profession. He had no doubt that he would be extremely wealthy in a very short time. If others were more conservative due to scruples, that was their problem. He had never been required to take a course in "scruples" for his MBA and they were not his concern.

Ron's eyes and total concentration were centered on the screen. He was watching the results of daily trading on the stock market. He worked at one of the largest investment companies in the world and he was very good at what he did. He studied the market with an intensity which truly impressed his superiors and his ability to predict biotech companies on the verge of being surprisingly good investments was starting to get him a reputation. He wanted to make the kind of killing which would give him the life to which he was entitled. He had several things cooking, if he could just take care of the details.

Ron's interest was in the biomedical and biopharmaceutical fields. What he was particularly good at was differentiating between which start-up companies could be a land of opportunity or a landmine. One had to be very careful about their investments. What irritated him was what seemed to be the ease with which a series of unexpected discoveries could catapult some collection of obscure scientists to wealth overnight. He had made it a major point of his day to watch very carefully the stock market. He also read the scientific journals, kept up with the biotech companies reported in the Wall Street Journal, the annual report of the big pharmaceutical companies, and tried to keep track of new fledgling biotech companies. What he needed to do and what he fully expected himself to do was to follow the scientific literature to not only get in on the "killings to be made" but to be in the front line in anticipation. To help him with this goal, he had spent every night on the internet reading everything he could about the new DNA revolution. He had started slowly learning the basics.

For his study, he simply acquired a college biology textbook and read. His reasoning was that if dopey freshmen with their distractions could master the stuff, then so could he. He was now familiar with the basics. He knew what DNA was and more importantly, he was starting to not only understand what could be done with DNA manipulations but also how easy it was to do so much of the work. He didn't expect himself to be able to design experiments but he was quite pleased with himself that he could approach understanding most of what he read, at least in review articles. He liked to think of the journal *Science* as a version of *Time* magazine with a heavy duty science section in the back. The gossip of the science professions was often presented in finely written accounts of grants mismanagement, dangers of academic dishonesty and comments on the policy-making aspirations of various members of the society which published the journal.

His eyes often lingered on the advertisements for so many products. What struck him was the sheer volume of products being directed towards the medical/biological field. It was very clear that biology and medical research was big business these days. No wonder there were so many investors willing to dump money into companies with products they didn't even understand. Yes, he had known that he would find his future in this area. He had struggled with his superiors to get them to focus on this area for such a long time. If they were not going to follow his lead, then he would take the lead himself.

He had taken careful note after the fact, of the rise of the most well-known biotechnology company, *Cellstart*. He had committed himself to learning about the progress of the scientists who founded the company. This had been his approach, to see how the science developed and then follow how the companies had been formed, their rate of progress and what pushed them into the public arena. He had wanted to anticipate the opening up of a company for investment. He had entertained no doubts that he could master what it took to carry this off. He had spent considerable time observing and researching the progress of three different labs which had been focusing on a novel approach to treating tuberculosis. He had followed a simple article in *The Los Angeles Times* which had detailed the arrival of a type of tuberculosis in Russian immigrant populations which wasn't responding to simple antibiotics. In fact it didn't seem to respond to any kind of antibiotics. A note of alarm had been present in the article but it had only triggered curiosity in Ron. Were there other diseases out there that were going to be trouble and how was the scientific community responding? He had come to the conclusion that antibiotics might be a thing of the past.

He wasn't about to invest in a pharmaceutical company specializing in antibiotics if they were not going to be effective for very long. What he had discovered in his two yearlong studies was that the scientists in the three labs were designing molecules to directly attack the weak point in the make-up of the toxins of the bacteria that caused the disease. All of this was possible because of the new technologies available. He had speculated that in this area, antibiotics were virtually obsolete and the newly engineered molecules were going to spectacularly alter medicine.

Early in the spring preceding the murder of Mike DesFleur, Ron was encountering the financial outcome of a course of action that had taken him into disaster. He had made a critical mistake. It was hard for him to admit that his intellect, which he considered to be immense, had failed him. How was he to know that the carefully thought out approach which he prided himself on, could lead him to the brink of professional ruin and financial distress.

Ron had placed the bulk of his own money into investing in a small biotech company which quietly and without big fanfare had prepared a drug to treat nerve damage. It had been so successful in small animal studies that Ron was feverish to back the company. He invested a quarter of a million dollars into purchasing the stock of the parent company. This amount in and of itself could have been absorbed by his company without any problems as it was, by industry standards, a small loss. If the company had known about it. However, he wasn't involving the company in this particular deal and he could not possibly have been expected to come up with that amount of his own money. He had placed the money of a client of his company in the deal as well.

Some clients were more flexible in their dealings and sought ways to invest without a lot of regulations in the way. Some clients had money to clean up or launder. All the transactions had been done circumventing the company he worked for. It had been a private venture, a side venture which he entered into knowing that he could lose his job. This did not stop him. If the company he worked for did not want to follow all his leads, then he would take care of business in a different way, his own way. How was he to know that what may be good for little rats and mice could be bad for humans? He had presented the risks to the investor and he didn't understand why the man was so angry, so very angry when the risk proved fatal. Ron had managed to do some fast talking and manipulation to protect himself from a client who was more than intimidating. The whole mess had left him somewhat depleted financially and now he had debts to pay to someone who had the capacity to hurt him, if not professionally, then physically.

Ron's life style was fairly typical for a young man on the way up. He worked a crazy number of hours which he referred to as "24-7" and at least until recently had amassed quite a bit of money. He didn't have time to spend it. He had no one to spend it on and considered his most romantic encounter to be the recognition of a possible money-maker for the firm's clients. His was a rather limited but driven life.

As he sat at the computer, his fingers tapped at a furious pace, either on the keyboard or on the table. He was nervous and concerned. He had financial obligations which were taking up more of his time than he wanted. He was trying to focus on his latest enterprise which if all went well, would re-instate him financially and professionally, at least in his own eyes. He would be able to pay off what he still owed his previous investor and he would be okay. Why this investor was so pissed off, was something he didn't quite understand. What Ron did not know was that this special investor had himself, used money that perhaps wasn't completely his to invest. Brazen in the face of the promise of large financial gain, his secret investor was now quietly dealing with panic and dread. Perhaps time would take care of these nasty little details.

Ron's plan had revolved around the Osaka-Health Pharmaceutical company. His father had worked in his professional life with one of the key executives and Ron had met him under circumstances which were more family-oriented than in the business arena. The executive had been most interested in his ideas and Ron started to actually envision what a life in Japan would be like. This company understood the risks involved in going into new territory. The more encounters he had with the executive, the more he realized that Japanese businessmen understood that sometimes the limits imposed by "legalities" were the creations of mere men and meant to be overcome by more clever men by whatever means presented themselves. His new approach would be more fruitful. He would have an ally who was in the labs and who followed the work done with special molecules. His ally would give him the edge which he himself was lacking. It would take care of everything. All he had to do was get some money to make even more money. This he could do. He was sure of it.

# CHAPTER TEN
## A LESSON IN DNA

**BRANDELL AND YVETTE SAT IN** the office on a bright Friday morning the second week in December. The holidays were approaching and the students were not as frequent weekend visitors as usual. The criminal investigation was going on full speed and Yvette and the detective were now on a familiar first name basis. On her desk, lay a pile of the unique laboratory notebooks which she had special ordered. Each one had a blue and gold University insignia on the cover and was bound on a spiral with each page numbered. Every page had a duplicate for making a carbon copy. Brandell thought the system was very sophisticated as well as organized.

"What I would like us to do is to re-examine the work which your students are doing. I want you to stretch your imagination and see if anything strikes you as off or not quite right. We could start with the most recent stuff."

Although Yvette grimaced inside at the thought of her students' work being referred to as "stuff," she understood what he meant and reached for the first notebook. Brandell extended his arm out and handed her Mike's lab book.

"I would really like it if you started with Mike's notebook"

Yvette opened the notebook with a queasy feeling in her stomach. What exactly was she supposed to look for anyways? She looked at the date on the opening page of what was his sixth notebook in her lab. She carefully and painstakingly read all the write-ups of the procedures, the results and stated observations of each experiment. This was all familiar territory. She kept close tabs on what each student was doing. She was particularly mindful of the temptation present for a young student who thought they could be doing better than they were. There would be no fraud in her lab because she was lazy. She read their work and met with each student regularly to see their progress. Mike's work seemed to be okay. His code words and abbreviations initials for cell lines and plasmids were all recognizable. She started to close the notebook and place it on the counter when Brandell reached out and took it from her.

"Sorry but this is still evidence. You'll be able to get it when we're through with this."

Yvette remembered the carbon copies of each page and asked if it would be alright to pull them out. Brandell raised an eyebrow and said

"I don't think so. This evidence is supposed to remain intact. When this is over, I'll see that if you can't have the notebook or the carbon, at least, you can photocopy it, Okay?"

Yvette responded as she reached for the next notebook.

"All right. Let me continue on."

Jolie's project was to examine the effects of several of the factors isolated in the lab, on her neurons in cell culture. Note page after note page described in detail repeated experiments introducing the first factor, GAGA, to the cells which were present in the most sterile conditions in the lab. Page after page described the neurons spreading out and making multiple connections with other cells. Jolie was right on course. Yvette remembered that the last time she had sat with Jolie and the notebook, the whole episode had given her a headache. Jolie was set in her ways and her ways did not include such trivial details as the date or even the number of the culture flasks she was using. She had an excellent memory and such details were always at her fingertips. Unfortunately, she had to be told repeatedly to slow down and document things better. Although she still had some glaring omissions, things had improved as of late and her notebooks reflected it.

"I can't think of the students doing dishonest things in the lab. It gives me the creeps." Yvette gave a frustrated look at Brandell and picked up the next notebook.

Slowly, she went through each of the student's lab books. Jolie, Rich and Mike all had pretty ordinary notebooks. Each one was on track.

"I really appreciate your time." Brandell said as he sipped his coffee. Knowing about DNA was okay and may or may not be really relevant to the case but right now, he was watching the professor. What made her tick? "I'd really like a primer in DNA again." Yvette reached for one of the textbooks which was on a shelf adjacent to her desk. It was an introductory book for College Biology.

"Where to start...now where to start....DNA is a molecule that is made up of two strands, like a rope" Yvette had said this bit so often she didn't want to sound like a robot. She carefully selected the appropriated diagram and picture from the text and checked with Brandell's face to make sure that he got it. Here was a student, unlike some students she had encountered, who was a novice and had a novice's curiosity. She continued on.

"The strands twist around and are held together by forces which the units have for each other in the strands. The strands, if they were just string or rope could pull apart quite easily, however, the force which holds them together is sort of like poor glue. It keeps the strands together but not too tightly. Each strand is made up of four different molecules and only the same four. We call them bases."

Yvette turned the page to a simplified picture.

"The sequence of the bases is the very secret of the whole works! The sequence is the directions or code for the cell to make everything it needs. Just as the dots and dashes of Morse code are limited in their sophistication, we can combine them enough to get our message across. Right?" She checked that he was following the text intently,

"In the case of DNA, we're talking about a molecule that has been with living things since the beginning of life or damn close to it. The whole DNA thing which you have been reading about in the press involves reading very large sequences of the code and deciphering what it means."

Brandell was trying to understand how money could be made from such information

"So, if one knew the code for something, like a drug or something, they could use that to make money?" It was a rhetorical question because Brandell didn't have a clue. "Those people who can figure out what kind of mistakes are in the code in different kinds of diseases, I guess, could make scads of money if they sold the information to a biotech company or something like that. We do not do that kind of research in the lab. The DNA business is big time, I mean, really big time. We're not in that league. You know what they will do with the information?"

Yvette continued on. "The erroneous code can be replaced with a corrected version and then placed inside the cells of the person suffering from this disease or that disease. It is really clever how they do this."

Yvette was really hitting her stride and took pleasure in explaining the complexity of it all. "They can make a piece of DNA in a machine now. They take it and combine it with a special kind of DNA already found in nature. This little DNA is made by bacteria, you know what bacteria are, right?" Brandell gave a nod and Yvette rolled on.

"Well bacteria make these tiny little pieces of DNA and give them back and forth to each other. We call them plasmids and they are useful for inserting a piece of man-made DNA into a receptive cell. The plasmid and a virus can do the same thing. So a plasmid is like a little carrier of a piece of DNA. Now plasmids, we do work with these little critters in the lab. They are very easily manipulated. Now I mean very, very easily manipulated. How easy? My students can do it. Our deep freezer, in fact our liquid nitrogen freezer, is full of them with all kinds of pieces of DNA inside them. Every time we identify a protein-based growth factor, we sequence the units which make it up and then we try to make a code for it out of DNA. We try to make a copy of the gene for it and store it in a plasmid. You know it isn't as mysterious as it seems." We have hundreds of plasmids in the freezer."

Brandell asked her if she routinely went through the tank to sort.

"Oh no, hardly ever. We spend so little time opening and closing the tank because it can cause the liquid nitrogen to dissipate. We have log books to know where everything is. It's not like you can open up the tank and go fishing. You need to know where you're going before you open the lid. It's just like the sperm banks. You know the folks that are looking for Mister Right have to know exactly where to look. They can't be fumbling around and accidently let Mister Wrong melt."

Yvette wanted to change the subject without seeming too inquisitive.

"Is there anything which would help you coming from your information about Mike's personal life? I mean, have your interviews found anything interesting? Somehow the thought of a bimbo bonking him one for infidelity just doesn't seem right. Perhaps in our day such a transgression would warrant a major response but not today. Young people are much more casual in their relationships, don't you think?"

Brandell smiled and answered "I see a lot of the handiwork of love gone wrong in my profession so I try to never underestimate the power of jealousy and anger. I wouldn't mind if I could consult on the case in a more serious manner. I must admit I am stumped a bit about motivation for something to happen in your lab and to this young man in particular. Let me check with the department so see what the "rules" are about such collaboration and I'll get back to you."

After Brandell left, Yvette felt a little pleased with herself. She could be part of the investigation. She guessed this meant she wasn't under the magnifying glass herself.

# CHAPTER ELEVEN
## COCKTAILS AT THE CANOE

**THE ONLY DEMONSTRATION OF ANXIETY** Ron Hattori displayed was the periodic rhythmic tapping of his fingers on the dark, scarred and ever-so-slightly sticky pine table. Quietly sitting in front of a whisky and ginger ale, Ron allowed his eyes to roam the tavern while he waited for his lunch-time companion. He sipped his drink with a slight resentment as he had really wanted a simple beer. He did not think it seemly however that he, a young Turk of the business world, would drink something so unsophisticated as a simple beer in public. The beer would have to wait until he got home.

Ron frequented the Canoe Club, a midtown bar located on Broad Street and within walking distance of his office. The decor was that of pseudo-hunting lodge for the pseudo-outdoor enthusiast. A rather impressive stuffed moose head loomed over the bar and various kayaks, skis, snowshoes and even a toboggan decorated the walls. A large handmade wooden canoe cut in half had been attached to the wall over the bar and Ron pictured the other half intruding into whatever establishment was situated there with some confused paddler stuck between the bar and a hair salon.

In a short while the lunch time patrons would show up and the place would be filled with young and neatly attired business people, mostly men seeking a lunch-time fantasy of being in the wild and dangerous wilderness of raw nature rather than the treacherous business world of their own making. Ron believed that these guys had probably never even sat in a canoe let alone actually survived taking one out on a river. For sure they had never even sat on a toboggan let alone used a kayak, his preferred water vehicle. Aside from the silly drinks in the bar with names like "Mojito Moose" and "Avalanche Ale", meant to attract the women, the food was pretty good and he could have a private conversation in one of the back booths where he now sat.

After a thirty minute wait, his partner in lesser known business affairs, arrived. Skip Chandler was a research scientist at *BIOFUTURE*. This was how he presented himself. In fact, he was a laboratory assistant in a lab which uncharacteristically gave him a bit of freedom to work at the bench not completely supervised. He was a tall, blond man with the build of someone who has made a niche for himself at the local gym. Skip had graduated the year before Ron had even arrived at the University. However Ron had made his acquaintance, first through the copious copies of old exams Skip had left behind as his gift to University life of his fraternity brothers and only later met him in person to thank him for all his help. Chandler was six years older than Ron but came with a singular impeccable credential which indicated he was trustworthy in every respect, he was a fraternity brother.

Skip made his way to the back booth repeatedly glancing at himself in the mirror behind the bar, making sure his blond ponytail was properly placed. He took it all in, he was more than presentable. Ron greeted his friend with "Where the hell have you been? I've been waiting for a half hour."

Skip barked at Ron without making eye contact, "I was busy and got caught up in something. I'm here now, so don't get all worked up about the small stuff,"

He then snapped his fingers to grab the attention of the waiter and called out his order

"Budweiser and some pretzels!"

Ron felt an immediate inner sense of smug superiority in his drink choice. *A domestic beer! Some people have no sense of appearances.* They exchanged the usual small time trite conversation while looking at the menu they knew line for line. Once their order was taken, the men lowered their voices and initiated the real reason for their meeting. Ron leaned ever so slightly across the table and spoke in a low voice.

"I had a visit from my personal investor. He's starting to put pressure on me to compensate him for my bad judgement. Although I think that the quality of my judgment is a matter of opinion, he wasn't interested in discussing the issue. To ensure that I understood this, he brought with him a gentleman who did not offer his hand in the intro and kept them folded in front of him as he stood in front of the door. His name was something like 'Mr.

Grey' or maybe it was 'Prey.' He was not friendly. In fact, he was downright creepy."

With this, he sat back and waited for a response from Skip whose face remained blank and appeared somewhat disinterested.

"And..." was the only word to come out of his mouth as if to say 'what is this to me?'

Ron licked his lower lip then spoke slowly and with deliberation in each word.

"It means that they are going to hurt me unless I give them something to quiet them down. Do you understand?"

Ron was at a distinct disadvantage but he didn't know it. Although he was in charge of the finances for the first part of Skip's plan, he wasn't to be involved in any other aspects. He was in charge of the set-up money, the agent who would find the cash to purchase equipment, pay the rent on the lab space and buy biological supplies. Skip's secretive and tight control of all the other details somehow was comforting to Ron. After all, Skip was a genius and the mind of a genius was something to respect and trust. Skip would work out all the scientific details and experimental data. He would get the contact to set them up in a real facility and he would do the presentation to get the investments to get company started. Ron was to stay out of the way.

Ron leaned in and with his eyes on Skip's asked

"What is happening on your end?"

Skip took a sip from his chilled beer.

"Well, I ran into a bit of trouble but it's been taken care of. I still have to get some things together. Now, at least I know where they are."

His eyes monitored the other people in the bar. He didn't recognize a soul and so he continued on.

"The winter break is coming up and I will be able to get what I need. The lab where what I need is, is going to be moved into a new building. There'll be some down time before this happens and that's when I will get back in and take what I need. See. It's very simple. It's under control."

Ron listened but his curiosity was piqued. Taking another sip of his drink he asked

"Can't you just ask them for the stuff?"

At this point, two separate parties of lunch patrons entered and the restaurant became more animated. This wasn't considered intrusive by the dining partners as it provided needed noise to drown out the details of their own conversation. Skip looked across the table and with very direct eye contact stated

"It really shouldn't concern you. It's taken care of. I'll let you know when I am ready to proceed with the work at the bench. Right now, I'm taking care of the preparation."

Ron was about to take the last sip of his whisky when a waitress appeared.

"Shall I bring you another round?"

Ron wasn't about to answer and validate her intrusion into their private and guarded conversation. He just finished the drink and placed the glass on the table. Skip on the other hand, produced a soulless faint smile and motioned with a raised thumb that they most certainly would like another set up. The waitress took the order and retreated while Skip allowed his face to assume its normal emptiness.

Ron, like a dog with a bone, would not let go.

"Is the *problem* something that is going to impact on me? Is it really something I should know about?"

He was less intimidated than he was concerned that some facet of the deal they were working on, had gotten out of control. Ron, himself, was a man of control. He also felt due to his superior gifts, that he was in control of many of the people around him. *They were so pathetic, the way they listened to him so intently, and the way they thought his ideas were so inventive. They didn't know the half of it. He was capable of telling them anything and they would believe him. It was just his convincing manner and the ease with which he could bend the truth to what they wanted to hear. What were lies to some, he believed must be the truth to someone else.*

Skip realized he now had an opportunity. Why keep secrets from Ron when telling him could be so useful! Ron could know something without knowing everything.

"There was an accident."

Ron took a deep breath, tensed his facial muscles, ignored a slight pang in his chest area and set his drink down on the table.

"What *exactly* do you mean?"

Skip's eyes were fixed on a party several tables away. A pretty girl had just arrived and it was obvious that the men were glad she had decided to join them. Skip focused on the maneuvering of the men while his conversation was directed across the table

"What the hell do you think I mean? Haven't you read the newspapers?"

The waitress brought their drinks and quickly left to serve other more boisterous patrons. Ron's face did not betray the speed with which his mind was working.

Thoughts were flying in and out of focus. He was resisting the urge to leap up and run out of the restaurant. *Was that lab killing related to Skip's work? Did he actually kill someone? Is this what "an accident" means? What is this to me? I didn't kill anyone. I don't know what he is talking about. Besides, if he did kill someone, it's too late to do anything about it. I'm not involved in this. I can take care of myself. He had better take care of himself as well.*

Ron now experienced a heavy and sickening feeling in his stomach. He had to control his response to this new development. He thoughtfully said "It seems to me that this part of the business is really not my affair. I'm not responsible for anything which was not part of our original agreement."

Their eyes were locked in a knowing moment, a moment in which their mutual fates were sealed.

Pony tail answered "As I was saying, I took care of business, my business. Now, you take care of yours."

The bar was now filling up with hungry customers. The two men ate in silence. Had a psychologist hovered above and listened to the two men, like the proverbial "fly on the wall" they would have thought the conversation worthy of any classroom lecture. The physical movement of the two bodies was a lecture in and of itself. With very little eye contact except for the most momentous parts of the conversation, and then only to challenge or threaten, hostility floating under a veneer of civility. Yes, the title of the lecture would be "Sociopath meets psychopath." for lunch.

# CHAPTER TWELVE
## THE FACULTY CONVENE

**YVETTE'S NEXT WEEK IN THE** lab was uneventful until Friday. Every other Friday morning of the month, the faculty met in the large departmental conference room. No issue was too little or too irritating to be ignored at the Friday morning experience. The Chairman of the Department, Peter Martin, was already seated at the long table, his coffee and notes ready for the onslaught. The table he and the others would sit at would have done any lawyer's office proud. The long oak wood surface had mellowed to a fine golden color and smooth in its finish. One could never even speculate over what the table had witnessed through the years. This would be like any other faculty meeting with prolonged discourse on trivia and short discussion of the more important matters which more than likely had already been settled in private discussions.

Yvette arrived early. She wanted to set up a meeting with the chair to discuss exactly where she would be able to have an office. She filled her cup at the prepared coffee table and helped herself to a muffin. She expected at any time, that the free coffee and muffins would become a thing of the past, sacrificed in the name of fiscal austerity. She took a seat at the table and sat quietly in her chair but her mind was distracted and racing. Could she take this for very much longer? How was it going to be possible to continue on in her life as if nothing had happened when this horrific event just sat there in her consciousness, screaming an obscene violation of her life, her work space, and her day to day escape from the ordinary? No, nothing was going to be the same. She would focus on sitting still, not betraying her inner turmoil and try to not run from the room screaming.

In came the cast of characters she knew so well. Professor Harper was talking with Tom who appeared to be listening but probably was displaying his mastery of the faux look of fascination. Helen talked animatedly describing the last committee meeting she co-chaired with a member of the physics department. Helen gushed on

"All they could talk about was the new building and who was going to be where. Honestly, it was very irritating. I'm more concerned about what we're going to be offering the students in the fall curriculum for the joint science symposium. I had a headache after the whole thing was over. I felt like I was pulling teeth to get them to focus."

With that she promptly plopped her round little body into a chair and started rustling papers from a folder she had brought with her. Tom gave Yvette a weird little smile, a sly wink and headed for the coffee urn. He took his seat next to Yvette. Yvette wanted to throttle the woman and ask her if she thought a murder would be more fitting as a cause for a serious headache. Professor Wolsey entered in his usual state of disrepair, head disheveled, the look of a "deer in the headlights" on his face. Brilliant he may have been but there was no doubt he was a strange guy. He never said very much but when he did, he was erudite, observant, and possibly in the possession of a wry sense of humor. Yvette liked him ever since he stopped by to introduce himself to her when she first arrived in the department. He apparently thought it was important enough to say hello and she never failed to greet him since that day. Yvette made a mental note to engage him in a conversation about retreating from the world of curious and intrusive colleagues. Perhaps he would have an insight about the academic world as a safe place.

Next, in came the "molecular mafia" as they were known by the other faculty whose bent wasn't DNA-oriented. These were three middle age men, whose constant companionship with each other made them almost appear as a single unit, voting the same on all issues, sharing the teaching of courses together with adjacent offices and generally, considered as mildly threatening to the rest of the faculty. They combined their efforts to create a whorl of discussion they dominated, to get the attention of the Division's version of the rich but tight-fisted Uncle Scrooge, otherwise known as the Dean. Yvette considered herself ahead of the game as she usually saw what was on the agenda with these guys. Today was no different, they were talking together, sat together and all looked at her together when she said hello to them. She allowed a single humorous thought to enter her head. What if this had happened in one of their labs? Her mental picture was of the hapless professor calling his colleagues to share the experience, less they be left out or misinformed, the three of them falling over each other to look at the body, each finishing the other's sentences as they decided what to do. Of course, they would be forced to figure it all out since everyone else would be so clueless.

She had been perfectly used to their cajoling of her, but she would have none of that now. She would hold her own whenever they started up and then she would go home with a headache. As expected as the three blind mice walking in tandem, the three professors took their seats together. Next, came the resident expert on neural growth factors and after him, the self-described expert on everything but who actually had a program focused on regeneration of injured cells. That was it with the exception of two faculty on sabbatical, two who were currently in the classroom and one who was nowhere to be seen. Lucky stiffs all!

After the usual exchanges of quick gossip and hellos, the Chair asked that everyone be quiet. He was ready to start with his agenda.

"Alright now, let's see, where do we start?"

He may have been asking, but Yvette told herself she would scream if he did not start with her situation. "We're all terribly traumatized by the death of a student here in our department. I know that it has been difficult to not know any more than we do. We can't do a damn thing about it except keep in touch with the police. I haven't a clue what they know so far."

"First order of business. Yvette what is happening in your lab now? Are your students in the lab?"

Yvette felt relieved on the inside. At least someone cared about her students. And "Yes", the students, still alive, were in the lab. "Well, we're starting to use the lab. I have expressly forbidden any students to be in the lab in the evening unless a second person is with them. I really don't think this necessary to tell them. It was hard enough to get them to come back in during the day, never mind the evenings or weekends. We do have all the cells in storage as well as in the incubators so, we have to get in to feed the cells as well as monitor the storage tanks. You know, the liquid nitrogen tanks. So, I guess we're slowly getting back to normal."

The Chair then asked her about the fall she took in the lab. "I don't want to be melodramatic but did you fall or were you pushed? You didn't say anything to me but I heard about it. I am concerned, so what happened?"

Yvette readjusted herself slowly in the chair, giving her a moment to think out the most prudent answer. Should she say she tripped and that only her paranoia made her feel like someone was in the lab or should she say she was pushed by someone who she did not see?

"Well, let's say that I was very nervous going into the lab and I had my hands full. You know I hadn't been able to get in there for some time while and I was starting to accumulate things at home that should have been in the office. I had a bunch of papers in my arms and was barely able to open the door with my key. I think I may have dropped something and tripped over it. I'm okay. Really, I'm okay." She looked at the collected faces of her colleagues and reassured them she was alright. They, as a group, had the collected look of not believing a thing she said.

Peter then exercised the prerogative of the Chairman. "Dr. Bilodeau, I am asking you not to use your lab like you're staying there indefinitely. The labs in the new Crick building are almost complete and ready to move into. Ribbon cutting is in two weeks. I want to talk with you separately and discuss your move into that building as soon as I am given the okay from the Dean's office."

Now that got everybody's attention. She could almost hear the hearts stop beating while the Molecular Mafia sat up to attention and zeroed in. *Who the hell was she to get first pick of the labs? So what if she had a lab with blood in between the cracks on the floor tiles.* Whatever system would be devised to get them all into the new building in the rightful places, would now have to wait until Yvette was sitting sweetly in her new lab and office.

She could feel what they were thinking.

"Labs should have been assigned by seniority or by lottery or some such method."

*"The lab spaces could have even been doled out with the unique needs of each lab as a consideration."* They would even go that far in their arguments against giving Yvette special consideration. She listened and took in more than she had expected. *No, this is going to change. I am still in the prime of my intellectual life. Why should I just have to listen to this crap and not have an alternative? Well I will find that alternative. I will experience some consideration and respect if it kills me.* The possibility of this last thought, killed the reverie and brought her back to the faculty meeting. The chairman was droning on about the new building

"The new building, will be named after Sir Francis Crick. An anonymous donor has made this stipulation and I know that the amount put into the building of the structure by this donor is in excess of fifty million. So it will be 'the Crick Building'. I know that there are always some comments about just how much Watson and Crick did, and their stealing or borrowing Rosie Franklin's data, but The Crick Building it is"

And with this he gave Yvette a slight little wink of the eye.

"The ribbon cutting will be, as I said, in two weeks. I know that some of you are disgusted that you were not in on the planning of the building and the labs. I do believe that perhaps we will be better off this way. The architects have recently finished the newest wing at the Salk Institute and they are really up to date on how to organize research areas. In fact, this was the draw for this architectural firm. They seem to have thought of everything and some things that I had not even thought of myself." Yvette allowed herself to ponder the thought of the architects planning on triple locks on the lab doors and overhead monitors of all hallways and lab spaces just in case of a threat of a repeat of that "horrible incident." *No amount of planning or building can protect you when you can't even imagine the most horrible thing happening. She would have to protect herself. She would draw herself closer to Brandell Young. He seemed to know about murder, death and criminality, things that she hadn't entertained in her thoughts before.*

"Please be patient and relax. It will be wonderful for all of us. All I can say is 'Thank our lucky stars for computers'. All those little computers with all their little computer parts have made a large number of generous gazillionaires who now want to share. We will happily take from them."

He had no sooner taken a breath after finishing his last statement when the group started in. Professor Olson, Mafioso #1, spoke first,

"Pete, when can we actually pick out our particular labs? I would like to be..."

At this point, Yvette took a deep breath and held it. She knew what was coming and didn't want to laugh out loud.

"...near my colleagues with similar needs as far as common equipment."

"Of course Ken, you know that there will be common usage rooms. It will be quite central for several labs. You folks are going to be in heaven, honestly."

Alan Wolsey then meekly entered in "Do we have to move?"

Yvette could feel the pain of this introverted and social recluse. He was probably the most comfortable when he was in his office or lab, sequestered away from the public and working diligently on his numerous projects which had proven so fruitful for him. She would remember to offer to help him move his stuff. She imagined Alan finding a dead body in the lab and then keeling over himself, a victim of an unplanned encounter with cruelty and the worse that humans have to offer.

Peter gave a curt reply

"Yes, we have to move. The building is to be converted back into some kind of administration building. They don't dare tear it down. It's too old and too many alumni have pleasant memories of the building. It would make a 'big stink'. You know what a 'big stink' is for the University's fund-raising endeavors...the touch of death!"

Professor Faraday (no relation to the other Faraday of historical scientific fame), Mafioso #2, then piped up. "When will we be given the chance to select the labs, exactly?"

A second remark by Professor DeSica, Mafioso #3, followed. "It hardly seems respectful to keep us waiting until the absolute last minute to see where we are going"

The Chair, raised a gentle open-palmed hand to quiet a possible growing storm, said

"Now, my friends, a Chair only has so much power. Even the Dean has limited power to exercise when it comes to these things. Please start thinking of moving your storage materials first and believe me I will let you know ASAP when I know. Don't go get your shorts in a knot about things that you can't do anything about. Please think positively about the move."

Yvette appeared to the others gathered in the room to be quietly composed. Perhaps a sabbatical would be nice. To get away would be very nice indeed. It would be allowed. Hell! it might even be encouraged. On the other hand, it is a curious thing to be dealt a hand like this. How could she just walk away. No, she would stay and she would tackle this problem like every other question which arose in her scientific life.

She tuned into the dialogue of her colleagues. She had to admit to herself that she felt a certain simpatico with Alan Wolsey. She had finally come to be comfortable in her space. Moving would be a big pain in the ass. What if she had wanted to stay put...well that was out of the question. Aside from the building probably being home to a library or student services office of some sort, the thought of her student's blood seeped into the floor would be ever in her mind, no matter how many times the floor had been treated with hydrogen peroxide to get the hemoglobin out. No, she would move and apparently, she would move first!

# CHAPTER THIRTEEN
## MY DOMAIN IS MY KINGDOM

**SKIP CHANDLER DROVE INTO THE** large parking lot adjacent to the entryway of BIOFUTURE. He parked his 1968 navy blue MG roadster in his assigned spot and made his way into the large glass and chrome foyer of the corporate science facility. Skip thought of his car as "vintage" in the sense that it was old. It was also heavily dinged, and kept running by constant trips to the mechanics. While the car was problematic, the image it presented was everything to Skip. After all it spoke to his good taste.

Harrison "Skip" Chandler was born into "good taste". The youngest son of a family of four boys, he had the benefit of his parent's considerable experience raising young males. His parents had early on come to the conclusion that there was no treatment or pharmacological intervention for a budding sociopath. Unexpected dead pets, innocent looks in the face of obvious guilt, a certain deadness in his eyes, the best they could come up with was distance. So, little Skip was sent to boarding school. Two boarding schools later, he went on to the University and lived far away from his parents who by this time were to be considered as obstacles to his success. From his parent's perspective, less contact meant more peace of mind. Little contact with any grounding influence his brothers might have afforded him, helped shaped him into the singular entrepreneur that he was. Sure of his way, confident in his intellect without a care for those who disagreed, he was seeking his destiny. The women would come later.

What was that destiny? The goal was to be as successful a business man as his father who had certainly made his way in the world of high finance. The apple does not fall far from the tree was one of his working mantras.

Skip made his way past executive offices and one of the laboratory wings. With his blond hair tied back in his usual ponytail, he was as cool as the cold sterile entryway. He passed the administrative desk agent and security people, gave a disinterested nod, held up his ID badge and proceeded to the wings which held the laboratories. He entered into one of the three labs dedicated to the Neurosciences. The particular lab where he spent most of his time was the lab dedicated to cell research. The lab benches were covered with white lab surface, gleaming glassware, and various pieces of equipment functioning with an almost silent murmur. BIOFUTURE would spare no expense in maintaining a lab if they were to make millions in the near future on one of their discoveries, hence the space where he worked was top of the line with the most expensive equipment. Skip wasn't convinced that this "discovery: would be in the cell research division however, at least not any discovery that the upper management would know about. His own personal venture was going to be more successful, he was sure.

He worked quietly and liked to maintain a low profile when visitors were guided through the lab. His demeanor was all business, intense, and focused. With a little amplification of his resume conveniently omitting the year at UCLA graduate school, and adding the forged writing of wonderful letters of recommendation, he had landed a coveted position in the company to which many of his fellow classmates aspired. He knew he had a gift for the work he was supposed to do and required little oversight. His long hours were viewed as an exceptional dedication to the work and corporate spirit. His long hours, however, were not viewed so benignly retrospectively by the professors at UCLA who threw him out of their graduate program. Their simple belief was that long hours are just fine and welcomed when you are actually doing the experiments you are writing up. Making up data, however, isn't allowed. Now he had learned his lesson, slowed down and actually did the work. He wanted to stay at BIOFUTURE as long as possible to achieve his ultimate goal. He believed his destiny was to discover the ultimate way to correct damage to nerves.

Skip's hours in the afterhours were not to be wasted. His immediate supervisor, Dr. Clark Simmons, wasn't always supervising and perhaps was a bit too trusting to say the least! His drinking problem clouded his vision with regards to Skip and in return, Skip covered Clark's ass. In the quiet of the still lab when others had gone home, Skip worked on his own project, a very sweet deal. The company paid him for his own work which they did not know about. It was this very project he was betting on. It was the basis for his future. He was assembling a private lab in a rental space nearby and it was in this new space that he was launching his new biotech company, NEUROMATCH. He was slowly gathering the needed equipment to have the lab at least look like a functioning lab. Ron's pitiful investment was all he had so far but he had plans for more input from perhaps other investors. Skip's plan was to have the space look like he had done all his work here and when the day came that the big guns came to check it all out, he would be ready. It was all part of his plan.

Skip's lunch with Ron had gone just about as expected. The beer was cold, the salad fresh and Ron as clueless as ever. He moved away from the lab bench and sat at a desk area to sip some afternoon tea. His mind was busy, very busy. He would deal with Ron later. Right now he had other concerns. He had all the right components for his masterpiece of an experiment. The experiment, once revealed to the world, would make him rich. His plan was to present the work at the next meeting of the Society for Neuroscience in November where he was sure to attract the attention of investors. Everybody who wasn't a twit, knew the importance of being able to restore broken spinal cords, Huntington and Alzheimer damaged brains. He was convinced that his work would provide a very important and key step to fixing what was broken. He was so sure of himself that he had already submitted an abstract of his work for consideration by the society. He had written his abstract emphasizing the clinical importance of his findings. He had a grasp of what was important. It was a good result and a spectacular visual presentation to capture the imagination of the always present future investors looking for the next breakthrough. He envisioned one of the big biotech firms offering to buy him out or to offer to bring him into the fold. Now he had to do the work.

He carefully went over the details of the experiment. He had made a special kind of chamber to grow brain cells. His manipulation of their environment should allow them to grow towards each other and make contact. His collection of various growth factors from other labs would make a rich soup for them to bathe in. He had added a twist by giving them a special molecule which would fluoresce when the two brain cells connected. He would look forward to the day when he would look under the microscope and see the little flashes of green. Plus it would make a terrific picture to show to future investors. He carefully prepared the immaculately clean area under the reverse flow hood where he would open his cultured cells and start his experiment.

He had to wait until his boss left for the day. The pure luck of having a drunk for a boss wasn't lost on Skip. In seven months his division was to be shut down, his boss was to be "retired" and he was to be reassigned. How did he know this piece of news? He read his boss' emails in the late evening hours. Clark had already checked out, he just hadn't stopped coming into work yet. He was oblivious to Skip as long as Skip didn't interfere with his afternoon ritual of reading the scientific literature and web-surfing. Clark thought it was curious that Skip wanted to buy some of the equipment with his own money but if that was what the kid wanted to do, well soon it wouldn't be Clark's concern at all.

Skip sipped his tea and let his mind wander over his recent events. His surreptitious forays into the labs of established scientists had all gone well until the most recent one. Why had that stupid blond student given him such a hard time? If he had just accepted what Skip's explanation for being in the lab, he'd be alive today. He wasn't quite certain that he hadn't made an additional unnecessary mistake in his going into the bitch's lab. He had to think about this. There was no way to connect any of it to him. Well that wasn't exactly true. He did get into the lab with a bit of help. He had an accomplice, an unwitting accomplice who hadn't had a clue of what was to follow. Rich Kelly hadn't realized that Skip was a forceful person who would take whatever action was necessary to achieve the task before him. Rich had accidently left his keys in Skip's car where Skip came across them. He had made a copy of the lab key and returned the keys like the good frat brother that he was. The rest was history, as they say! Still, this was a detail which needed to be addressed. Rich had kept his mouth shut and hadn't been the focus of any attention just yet, but it was just a matter of time. What could he possibly say? He may not have even known that the key had been "borrowed." What to do? What to do?

When his boss departed for the day, Skip moved to the tissue culture hood and started adding his growth factors to the cells. Meticulously working, he treated the cells like the little gems they were. He carefully documented everything in a special notebook which he took home and worked on until after 1:00am. Success was just around the corner. He was sure of it.

# CHAPTER FOURTEEN
## TOO BIZARRE FOR WORDS

**ON A BRIGHT MONDAY AFTERNOON,** Brandell was sitting at his desk reviewing his file on the case which had remained unsolved despite the intense attention of both himself and his colleagues. His phone rang and he hesitated in picking up the line. There were other detectives lolling around. They could take it.

"Hey, Brandell, pick up on line two" Joe Madigan called from across the expanse of the empty detective's room. "I'm pretty sure it's for you...has to do with that University murder."

Brandell reached for the phone and listened attentively as the patrol officer informed him of a most unusual situation involving someone that Brandell most certainly would be interested in.

"Hi Detective Young. It's Rob Lark. I'm one of the guys who were with you when you went out to the University for that murder. I remembered the names of the students and when this name came up, I thought of you. Perhaps it's a coincidence but I thought you should know. We're down here on Wilshire and 20<sup>th</sup> at the sushi restaurant, "Sushi

Haiku." You know the one, the restaurant with the black front. Well, we got a call about a man sitting in his car for what seemed like hours. We were asked by the restaurant manager to check it out. Can you get over here?"

"Well, what exactly is the problem that I need to be right there?"

"He's just non-responsive to us and I thought you would want to know. His name is Richard Kelly."

Brandell took a deep breath and said "Okay, I'm close by. Just secure and wait at the scene."

It only took Brandell about five minutes to get to the restaurant parking lot. There were a half dozen people standing around all focused on the parked car. An ambulance had arrived and the attendants were examining the young man.

Brandell looked in the car and saw Rich Kelly. The young man was sitting up in his car with his hands firmly grasping the steering wheel. His eyes appeared to be focused on some distant point. His face had a slight grimace that wouldn't have been noticeable unless you knew what he normally looked like. Brandell had been to this place many times and recognized the man who he had always assumed was the manager. He called Seiji over with a slight gesture of his hand.

"Did he eat here today?"

"Oh, I think he did but I don't wait on the patrons so I am not sure. Let me ask inside."

He disappeared through the oversized black door, quickly returned, and asked Brandell to come inside.

"This is Maseo. He thinks that he waited on him very early for the lunch time. Around 11:00am."

Maseo had retrieved from the kitchen all the stubs he had generated with various patrons' orders. He was carefully combing through them to try to jog his memory.

"I think this is it. Party of two, sat in the last booth, one sake, one Corona, Sushi luncheon and sashimi dinner....yes I am pretty sure this is it."

Brandell then proceeded to ask the young waiter if he could describe the two men.

"Well, of course there was this one" which he indicated with a flip of his wrist vaguely in the direction of the parking lot. "And there was the other guy who has come in here before. He is a tall guy with a long blond ponytail. Nothing unusual about them really. They just ate and talked. I really didn't hear anything unusual."

"Okay, well thanks. If the Ponytail comes in again, call us. Here is my card." Brandell left the restaurant and saw the ambulance pull out of the driveway. First a murder in the lab and now this. Oh, no. Coincidence wasn't very big on his list of reliable phenomena.

On the afternoon of the next day, Yvette sat in the too warm departmental conference room with her colleagues and listened carefully to the Chairman describe various aspects of the big move. Yes, amazingly the entire department was going to be a state of the art research facility. She knew the devil was always in the details so she had to focus on what was being said. She had already begun moving her lab and students into her new space and was almost finished. She had yet to move the freezers and centrifuges but all was to be done in due time. She could not believe the splendor of the new lab. It was bright, airy and big! It also did not have blood on the floor and the haunt of a murdered student. The students would have plenty of space to spread out and there would be room for all the equipment to be placed in an organized manner. Yes, this was a research scientist's dream. It was also a dream to replace a nightmare. The Chairman had just started describing the movement of the centrifuge equipment when the departmental secretary peeked through the door and announced

"There are two policemen here and they wish to speak to Yvette."

Yvette's reverie was broken, her stomach had a slight twinge and she excused herself from her colleagues. Once in the corridor, one of the policemen gently took her arm and informed her that she was going to the police station for a little chat. Yvette's face flushed, her mind drew a blank and she allowed herself to be escorted out of the building and into a waiting police car. This had to be a friendly invite, but where was Brandell? Her mind drew a blank as to what could be the problem. She just sat there quietly until she reached the station. She had never been in a police station and was curious in spite of her anxiety. Busy people, some in uniforms others not.

Yvette was seated in a brightly lit room with several chairs located around a table, a coffee pot nearby and a large one way mirror on one wall. She was puzzled as to why she was here. Her mind raced as to what it all meant. Detective Young then entered and she felt a wave of relief and safety.

"Thank goodness you're here. What's this about?"

Brandell sat down, gave her a look without betraying a single emotion and asked her a single question,

"What do you know about Rich Kelly?"

Yvette looked at the detective blankly and said quietly and methodically reading a mental list. "Well, he's a student of mine. He's okay, right? You didn't call me because something happened to him?"

Yvette sat in the chair seemingly very calm but her heart was pounding.

"He is about to finish up his Master's degree thesis. He's actually at the writing stage. He isn't my favorite student. We never did gel as student and mentor. I viewed him as aloof and not warm to the other students. His work was alright. He was bright enough but not good with other people. That's about it. Oh, and he never was one to socialize with the other students. You know how students go out for a drink after work is done in the lab...well he was never really a part of that. I guess he had his own life elsewhere. Why are you asking about him? Has something happened to him?"

Brandell then sat down across from Yvette and kept his eyes directly focused on her face, waiting for any telltale sign of something out of the ordinary. "Mr. Kelly was found today sitting in his car outside a restaurant. Now this in itself isn't unusual." Brandell continued on in a slow paced manner. "However, he had been sitting like that for over three hours when some of the patrons of the restaurant who saw him as they entered to eat, also saw him in the same position when they left hours later. His hands were firmly fixed on the steering wheel like he was driving the freeway and he was staring ahead."

"The restaurant people called us when they could not get any response from him. They tried to connect with him to see if he was all right and to get his attention and he just kept staring right ahead. So they called us. Our officers approached him, got no response and he was removed from the vehicle. He's now at County General."

Brandell shifted in his seat and was watching Yvette's face as he went on.

"He did not appear to have had a stroke or other medical event which was easily recognized. They did however take a blood sample and checked for any kind of drug reaction. That was what they expected to find. However, they found something else. They found a very rare chemical in his blood. In fact, they were so surprised by what they found that they required a second sample and sent that one out to be tested by another facility. Yvette, tell me what you know about tetrodotoxin."

Yvette's face lost all color, and a look of fear and horror came over her.

"We have it in the lab!"

It was an admission she freely made and yet felt all of a sudden guilty about.

"It is a very powerful agent which has a very specific function in cell and biochemical studies. It is to be handled with extreme care as it can do a lot of damage in the nervous system. We have it in the chemical desiccator in the freezer and I can't think of when we would last have used it."

Yvette's eyes lost here focus and she seemed to be looking at a far off place where the memory of the tetrodotoxin's last use would pop up .

"I am pretty sure that most Neuroscience labs would have it on hand. It's not expensive and freely available through quite a few of the big chemical suppliers. It's definitely not for human consumption."

Brandell then asked her how a person would come in contact with it.

"Well, I don't know. It's not a drug like cocaine or any of the amphetamines or opiate derivatives that would be drugs of abuse and available on the street. You don't get high on it. Tetrodotoxin is dangerous and an experimental tool, not a drug of abuse."

She paused and then said,

"I am sure we have it in the freezer in the lab and"

Brandell then finished her sentence.

"Yes, and now we have it in our lab. We're looking at it for any comparison to what was in Mr. Kelly's blood. You know that these drugs often have contaminants allowing them to be recognized and differentiated by their sources. Tell me about the physical effects of the drug."

Yvette now made a decision which would take her into bizarre territory.

"Tetrodotoxin is pretty cheap as chemicals go because it's a biological product of puffer fish. The puffer fish as well as some kinds of newts and octopus exude this slimy film which contains the toxin. The puffer fish of course has it in high concentrations in their liver. It keeps them from being eaten while they are concerned with mating. This particular circumstance isn't lost on the natives of Central America who practice a different kind of "medicine." This is one of the poisons which make up the little bag of goodies used by the medicine men or shamans of Haiti. Now, I know that this isn't very scientific. In fact, it is embarrassing to even say it out loud, but it has been documented that tetrodotoxin along with some other hallucinogens like *Datura* are used to make people into, okay, I am going to say it, "zombies".

At this point, Brandell raised his eyebrows and interrupted. "What is a zombie exactly in your most scientific language?"

Yvette then drew from her memories of reading about ethnobotany.

"Well, a person given the potion is listless, has no inner drive or will power and will do as they are told. They can appear to be dead. You will recall the folk lore and Hollywood's portrayal of zombies is that they are presumed to be the dead come back to life. The folks who use this kind of "magic" do so to punish someone or do it for revenge. The person is drugged, perceived as dead, buried in a shallow grave and then dug up while still alive after the mourners are gone. They could then be sold off as a slave to someone else at a distant village. It is all very bizarre."

"There was a well-known book published by a Harvard scientist who actually went and studied in the jungles of Haiti and who documented the concoctions made of what we would call "tail of newt and eye of frog." He watched them prepare these potions but stopped short of seeing them actually give it to someone. It was bad enough he had to see them hanging dead animals to rot before doing their extractions. They may have played on people's superstitions but they did get the tetrodotoxin right! It does render you helpless and totally at the will of another. Quite a powerful drug. I don't know how long it is active. Maybe we could call the guy at Harvard and ask him!"

Brandell looked at this scientist, sitting before him and could not believe that she would administer a toxin to a student. On the other hand, she had actually brought up the term "zombie." Call it his professional acumen or just opinion, he would let her be for right now. Rich Kelly wasn't talking to any one so no one knows what this was all about. A call to Harvard might be just the right thing to do. Perhaps the ethnobotanist would have some insight into how long this stuff worked or if there was something to do to reverse it. He'd make the call this afternoon.

Rich Kelly with his mind a total blank, had gone quietly into the ambulance, gotten into the hospital bed and was undergoing a psychiatric evaluation. He continued to stare ahead with no words coming out of his mouth, no accusations or witnessing of evil deeds.

# CHAPTER FIFTEEN
## THE BIG MEETING IS COMING

**YVETTE SAT IN HER HOME** office reviewing all the abstracted material her students had produced and submitted to the Neuroscience Society. Every year she and her students went to the biggest scientific meeting in the country. It was an entire week of meeting with old friends for the most intense science exposure one could hope for. It was exhausting and thrilling. She and her students would be attending again this year. Usually, she and the students would travel all over the States for the meeting but this year it was right in Los Angeles. Everyone from the lab would go to the meetings, graduate students and undergraduates alike.

As she slowly reviewed the work her students had organized, her mind was distracted by a nagging thought. Someone with scientific savvy had stolen from her. The simple question was "Why?"

While she mulled this over, the phone rang and jangled her nerves.

"Hello, Dr. Bilodeau. It's me, Lili." Lili's voice was

shaking. "I am so sorry. Oh, I am so sorry! I made a mistake. I went into the liquid nitrogen tanks and found two of the four vials which I thought were missing. Now there are only two missing. One is the one numbered *H35*. It's the protein. The other is *Plasmid 5620*. I am so sorry if we misled the detective."

Yvette was doing mental gymnastics to place *H35 and Plasmid 5620*. Of course, it was the *"helper"* factor, *H35* and the DNA plasmid which contained the gene for the protein. This factor was a little quiet gem which she was working on in the lab but which she hadn't introduced to the neuroscience community. For the time being, it was a quiet little scientific secret. She only had one student, Rich Kelley working on it. It had quite the potential to help in neuronal repair and now two important vials were missing.

She couldn't help but wonder "the why" and furthermore "the how" these vials were identified. Now they were gone. A theft like that had its meaning. She just had to figure it out. *Who knew about helper besides her lab? Only people in the lab.* It was just too much to think about. What could it do without other factors working with it?

She comforted Lili and said it was all right. She was glad that Lili was so conscientious to go back and check the number and identity of all the vials. She said goodbye with the reassuring words of "it's all right, don't worry about it. I'll take care of it."

Now she was bothered both at the offense of the theft but also at the puzzle of what could be done with this factor by someone else outside her lab. She was pissed off.

She made herself a cup of hot tea and sat in her office at home staring at an empty computer screen. She wondered if someone had actually used her factor and actually was intending to present the work at the Neuroscience meeting. The meeting was a powerful presence in every neuroscientist's life. Careers could be made with a forceful and convincing presentation on one of the hot topics of the day. Chicanery could be exposed and careers permanently derailed.

She decided that while she wasn't an investigator of criminal activity, she had skills. She was a scientist. Didn't scientists search for the answers to questions, search the unknown and make educated guesses?

Yvette turned on her computer and logged on to the Neuroscience Society site. Years ago when she just entered the Neuroscience field, all the abstracts were compiled into a big thick book, the size of a telephone book. It had taken hours to comb through. Having all the information online shortened the time to find something of interest. It was a fabulous improvement.

How would she start? Well, now that was a question. She started with the broadest category, "cell culture" and got 5630 entries. She entered a new refining term, "neuron" and the 5630 entries were now reduced to 3998. How would she ever look at 3998 abstracts? She wouldn't and that was that. Forget that strategy. She was thinking that this approach may be a useless exercise.

She sat back, closed her eyes and let her mind rest and wander. *Whoever broke into the lab most likely is in the "neighborhood"* Of course the "neighborhood" was hundreds of square miles in Southern California.

She took a plunge and started all over again. She typed in "California" waited as the 1120 entries came up. So the number of abstracts was being reduced but still was very high. She saved the search as "Search California." While she waited for the computer to do its thing, the doorbell rang.

Yvette opened the door to Brandell Young. He looked tired and perplexed but she didn't know him well enough to even guess if this was his usual mood when working on a murder case. She was surprised to see him at her home and could think of no reason for him to be there that wouldn't be awful.

"Dr. Bilodeau, I need to speak to you." Yvette was a little alarmed at the formality of Brandell's tone but invited him in.

"I just need a few moments. I am on my way to the restaurant where we found Mr. Kelley. No point in looking for an antidote. Rich Kelley is dead." Brandell kept his eyes on Yvette's face. She returned his gaze with a blankness and a face totally devoid of any affect. Her mouth was open but no words were coming out.

"He never really regained full consciousness. A nurse in the room thought she heard him say a single word before his last exhausted breath. She thought he said "brother" but she wasn't sure. Kelly didn't have a brother, did he?"

Yvette quietly said, "Rich Kelley didn't have any siblings as far as I know."

Brandell continued on "The toxin didn't come from your lab in any case so he didn't dose himself! I thought you should know. You might also like to know that we didn't find his lab key in his home or on his key chain. That is curious but not unimportant. Even though you are moving out of the lab soon, I want you to change the lock on the door".

Yvette sat stunned. *Change the lock! Is he kidding? I'm never going into that space again.* When he left after dropping this latest bomb, she turned off the computer and the office light and sat in the dark space. She slowly got up, went into the bathroom and vomited.

# CHAPTER SIXTEEN
## BRANDELL HAS LUNCH

**THE NEXT MORNING AROUND ELEVEN** o'clock, Brandell arrived at the big black door of the popular "Sushi Haiku." The two other agents he had with him wore navy blue wind-breakers with the words "crime lab" printed on their backs. It was just before opening but this did not stop him from tapping loudly on the front door. The manager, Seiji Kogura, aggressively opened the door to announce that they were not ready to open. His face tightened when he saw Brandell and grew worried and confused as the two other gentlemen entered as well.

"Yes Detective. What is it you need from us? Come in, come in." Better to have them inside the restaurant before it opened than standing outside where others could see them.

Brandell walked past the manager and sat down at the sushi bar.

"Well, we have a little problem which can be solved with a little bit of cooperation. These two gentlemen, who he didn't bother to introduce have the special skill of being able to test for things. Now I would like them to test for something of interest in your kitchen. We can do this really quickly, say in about an hour, or if you would want us to return with special paperwork, we can shut down the restaurant for three or four days and do the testing."

The manager stood stunned and couldn't think of what the detective was looking for. "Can you tell me what you are looking for?"

The detective took a deep breath and said "fugu'. Seiji gasped and quickly let loose a flow of words characterized as "Deny! Deny! Deny!"

"We do not serve fugu here. It is very dangerous and we do not serve it here." He repeated himself quickly and adamantly.

Brandell then said, "Well, we'll see about that. I wanna speak to your sushi chefs while the boys here check out the refrigerators, the storage areas, the whole fish you have stored. All that is in the kitchen. Right now."

The manager backed into the kitchen and called to the three chefs to come out. He turned to Brandell. "The shortest one, Ryoto, likes to think he is a Sushi chef but he just cleans the fish. The tallest is Takumi. He can take a slice of tuna and turn it into a flower. He is my most special chef. The third one is Goro and he specializes in preparing the vegetable flowers. He also serves the customers."

"Well let's start with Takumi." The middle aged man looked warily at Brandell and slowly came into the bar area. The manager told Brandell that he would have to interpret since he did not speak English. And so the interview started. "Seiji tells me that you are an accomplished sushi chef. I have great respect for that, I really do." He was trying to put the guy at ease. Meanwhile Tacoma's eyes were staring without any sign of emotion.

"Do you prepare Fugu for the guests?" Brandell just hit him with the question without any pussy-footing around. Tacoma's face still did not betray any emotion but he looked at the manager and then blurted out,

"I am an accomplished sushi chef. Of course, in Japan, I prepared fugu. But there are many laws about this fish. We could no longer offer the liver which is filled with poison. It became illegal. I quit preparing the fish because of the clients who wanted it. Loud, boisterous, drunken businessmen trying to impress their friends and the women. College students, too drunk to even know what they were eating. It was obnoxious. Also, it was unnecessary. We have wonderful fresh tuna, shrimp, salmon and lots of other fish. Most people don't even know about fugu or the stories about fish poison. I do not prepare it anymore, never."

Brandell listened carefully to the soft spoken yet firm voice of the middle aged man as the manager connected the two men. "A customer who had lunch here one week ago, died of tetrodotoxin poisoning. Fugu poisoning." If we find that he ate fugu here, we will be looking at some very serious criminal charges. Do you understand?"

"I have nothing to be afraid of. I do not cut fugu. We do not serve drunken college students or old men trying to impress their women." The chef spoke slowly about the preparation of the fish, the cutting of the flesh with special care not to touch the liver, the tingling sensation that came with the fish and the single death he knew of in Japan before he came to the States.

"I knew of a single case, involving a young and arrogant

sushi chef at a small bar near where I worked. His workplace was near the Japanese financial district, Nihombashi, in Tokyo. The bar had many patrons in the later hours of the evening. Men who worked in the financial business. Men who overworked and played hard too. Too much sake and too much pressure to impress a boss who tagged along for an after dinner drink. My friend was asked to prepare the special fish. He at first said no but they kept repeating their request, getting more aggressive and loud. He overestimated his own ability but the lure of a big donation from the drunken men was too much to ignore. So he cut the fish trying to be careful. But as I said, he wasn't as good as he thought he was. He must have nicked the liver where most of the poison is, because the men were very impressed with the immediate tingling sensation of the fish in their mouths. One gobbled the fish up, pushing the hands of his fellows away. He was greedy. He sat for a few minutes and then fell off his chair. It was only due to the medical people that he made it. They pumped his stomach, I think. I don't serve fugu."

By the time he had finished talking about the fish, the two lab men had returned from the kitchen.

"We didn't find anything here. Not in the refrigerators, the storage areas or on the cutting boards." They kept their clip boards and small work suitcases and exited the restaurant. Brandell left with them momentarily and then returned inside.

"Thank you for your cooperation. Now, are you opened for lunch yet?"

The manager looked puzzled and replied that they

were. He motioned to the opened Black door and the entrance of a group of the early lunch crowd.

"Good, then I would like some lunch too. How about some sashimi?" He sat down at the bar and looked at the menu.

The little smile on his face wasn't lost on the manager. "And while you're at it, could I have a side of fugu?"

# CHAPTER SEVENTEEN
## THE PRIDE OF OWNERSHIP

**SKIP BOLTED OUT OF BED** at 6:30am when his alarm sounded. He had prepared for this day by taking a "personal day" off from the lab at *BIOFUTURE*. He got dressed, left his house in a flash and started up his sports car. Winding his way down the Hollywood hills, he felt giddy with excitement. He got on the Ventura freeway and headed west toward Thousand Oaks, the site of many biomedical companies and home of the mother of them all, AMGEN. The ride was marked by quick lane changes, excessive speed, and a certain recklessness which he tried unsuccessfully to keep under control. After forty five minutes of listening to Led Zeppelin, he signaled to turn off the freeway and continued for another three miles on surface streets. Finally he had reached his destination, Tech Drive. He pulled into the long driveway which served a long low series of individual business units. His was number forty three. There was no sign near the entrance but that would come in time. He had a lease for eighteen months and had spent no small amount on it. He put his key in the door and entered his new life. The space was a suite of three rooms; a large center room and two smaller side rooms. Sitting in the middle of the major room was a collection of boxes. The management had been kind enough to take them in when they arrived by UPS. Some furniture had arrived prior to this trip and had already been set up. The long central lab bench was ready for placement of equipment.

One of the side rooms had a laminar flow hood and had been set up to house his tissue culture supplies. He had set up the cell cultures here and placed them into the incubator, another pricey object purchased used. The room had a $CO_2$ tank and refrigerator. Skip was ready to move another set of his cultured cells from *BIOFUTURE* to his own lab here. He would do that in a few days. Right now he had to get all the equipment plugged in and working.

The main room had an Olympus UV microscope set up and this was the prize of the room. He had spent $15,000 for this scope buying it used from a local company that negotiated the resale of scientific equipment accrued from failing companies. He walked over to the scope and ran his finger over the objectives and the stage feeling elation at his good fortune in finding it. He started to move some of the newly arrived supplies into the tissue culture room. He moved boxes of culture plates and placed the culture media into the refrigerator. He had a small wall cabinet with various chemicals sorted and lined up. All of the supplies had cost him a pretty penny but only part of it was his own money. Ron had come up with a sizable chunk just in time.

Skip lovingly opened each of the newly arrived goods, like a child on Christmas morn unwrapping presents. He placed the small pieces of equipment on the bench top; a small scale, a heating block with a magnetic stirrer, a rocking water bath. He looked around and saw that he had, on a very small scale recreated his work space from *BIOFUTURE*. It was obvious that he had moved to the next level of his plan. A man like himself, a man destined from acclaim, could not be deterred from his fate by small quotidian events.

While he worked unpacking the latest shipment, he became aware that he wasn't alone in the room. Turning around, he was surprised to see the manager standing in the entryway. *How did he manage to get in so quietly and more to the point, was he going to be intrusive and, therefore, a problem.* Skip contorted his face into what would be recognizable as the face of a busy man who didn't need to be interrupted at this moment.

"Well, what can I do for you? And thank you for taking this equipment in for me. I don't think that it will be necessary for you to do that again. I certainly do appreciate it." Skip was waving between irritated and smarmy. He didn't need to irritate this guy and he most likely would need him again but he didn't need the idle curious.

"Just stopping by to see that everything is okay and to see if you need anything. By the way there are two other young guys with startup labs in unit thirty seven and sixteen, if you need anything." Bob Willet was intrigued by the confidence and energy of the young men. He was amazed at the whole biotech environment of what had been previously been a sleepy Los Angeles suburb. In his time, he had seen AMGEN come up and change the world. Now, the hopeful wannabees were showing up with an idea and some back up money. It was just plain mysterious as far as he could tell how they would make it.

"Well, I am just fine and thanks for the info. I really have a lot to do if you don't mind." Skip wanted him to go away. Bob took his cue, raised his hand in a salute and left just as quietly as he had come in.

Skip continued to move around the lab. He had moved a small desk into place and had a small lap-top computer on it. A phone had been installed under the name C. Harrison, a simple reversal of his real name. He wouldn't be known as "Skip" around here. He worked for the better part of the day, with each minute a glorious adventure. He mused that some scientists older than him would never have this much going for them.

He stopped cleaning, unpacking, storing, plugging in and checking out the cells in his new space and finally sat down. He had a simple task he thought would be totally enjoyable but was now giving him a headache. Of all the aspects of this venture which would prove to be a pain in the ass, doing the simple paper work was the worst. He had to have incorporation papers drawn up but more importantly, to make new business cards. His company was called "OMEGA SCIENTIFIC." The significance of the name wasn't to give illusion to the end of his scientific life but rather a private nod to one of the Greek letters of his fraternity. The meeting was just a few weeks ahead and he needed to be able to work the scientists that he had cultivated since last year.

As he waited for a small coffee pot to do its magic, he stared at the singular poster of DNA on the wall. It was a relic from a previous time, depicting the double helix in technicolor. While his eyes seemed to be focused on the artwork, his mind was wandering to last year's meeting. Skip had attended the meeting in Chicago under his C. Harrison persona. The crowds of scientists numbered in the thousands and yet he had managed to meet the kind of men he needed to contact for his venture. He had prepared for the meeting by culling from fifteen thousand abstracts, the three dozen which were of interest to him. Anything which dealt with neuronal repair was of interest. He eliminated all presenters who were strictly academic.

He focused on presentations sponsored by biotech companies. Academics had no money of their own so they would not be interested in dealing with him. Biotech companies or pharmaceutical firms were another story. The business world wasn't the same as the academic world. Yes, the commercial scientists, as he liked to call them, were a different breed. While the academics were hysterically happy to share every detail of their work, feeling obligated to pay back the populace for supporting their work through National Institutes of Health and National Science Foundation grants, the biotech folks felt no such compunction. Like winning poker players, they kept their cards close to their chests and only shared the most obvious scientific results. One could even go so far as to say that they went to meetings to gather up the fruits of other's labor and shared very little of earth-shaking quality. They had investors to please.

Skip had methodically noted when each abstract was to be presented. He chose those that were poster talks instead of oral presentations since this would allow him to actually meet the scientists and make contact. He had gone to each of the posters, studied the data, introduced himself and sized up the men he spoke with. They were mostly men since he didn't want anything interfering with his goal. Women scientists were a slightly different breed to him, more serious and perhaps distracting. He had found three men who were likely to listen to his offer. He had spent quite a bit on high end dinners and quite a bit more on bar tabs. The end result was three "contenders".

His presentation was seductive, intending to draw them into a deal. Skip spoke of spectacular findings he said were too precious to be generally announced. He was on the verge of releasing some of the data but he was very much interested in having the work developed commercially. What kind of company could resist the opportunity to be in on the ground floor of a major advance in repair of spinal cord injury, neuronal repair in brain damage! It would make billions. He put it out that he wanted to "join" a bigger company. He wasn't in the position to do it himself. He would need a bigger company to take him over. He had promised each of the three men that he had selected them because of their senior status in their companies, their scientific accomplishments and their obvious capacity to grasp the importance of what he was presenting. An ordinary person would probably sicken at the duplicity but Skip held different standards. He lured the men with a picture of future fame and fortune. He had picked men like himself. He courted them by email with frequent "progress" reports, promising each that they were the "one" to get the most up to date info. He had set in motion a process which was now full blown. He would go to the meeting in the Convention Center in the most quiet and understated manner, offer them the opportunity to see his work. He would invite them to the small lab of OMEGA SCIENTIFIC where he anticipated dazzling them with his results. He would then tell them of the interests of others in his work, a step towards making them feel pressure to bring the work to the attention of their superiors, if they had not already done so. No exaggeration was beyond him. He knew that he could do what he said he had already done. He would just have to get going. He now had just a few days to prepare for the meeting and perhaps a few months before he would reel them into his net.

# CHAPTER EIGHTEEN
## SKIP'S FULL DAY

**THE NEXT DAY, SKIP ARRIVED** at work an hour late and plopped down into the chair at his desk. He rubbed his eyes and gave a swift hand-pass through his hair. He gathered up the strands that had fallen in disarray the previous night and gave himself his standard ponytail. *If only sleep would come, he'd be okay. If only he could stop his mind from thinking of the details of every experiment, he would be okay. Working all day at the lab that actually paid his salary while putting in long nights at OMEGA which not only did not pay his salary but actually cost him an arm and a leg! How long can this go on? The annual meeting is coming soon, then it will stop.*

Skip turned on his computer, got himself a cup of coffee and stared at his email. There was nothing special in it. While he tried to get himself up to speed, his boss approached his desk, made a quick turn around and left the room just as abruptly as he had entered. On another morning, Skip, out of a sense of self preservation, would have sought him out to see if he needed something, but this morning he wasn't up to it.

After an hour of reviewing his notes from the previous day, he finally moved into the larger lab area and looked for his boss. Clark Simmons had seen better days for sure. When Skip found him at his desk, Clark was sipping some coffee which Skip knew contained Irish whiskey. He could smell it. He hardly raised his head to acknowledge his lab tech and mumbled something Skip couldn't hear or grasp.

"Clark, what's up?"

"Well, it sure as hell isn't me! I just got canned. Another six months to retirement and I got canned today. Oh, they said I would get my full retirement and I could hang out for the six months if I wanted to, but what the hell.... This is what I do every day."

Skip's brain was doing mental gymnastics with the skill of an Olympian, only he wasn't thinking about Clark's situation. *What would happen to him? Would he be transferred to another division or let go? Have they already got someone to replace him? What did all this mean to him?*

He started to open his mouth and decided to keep it shut and go back to his desk. He needed to think this one out. Clark's mental absence from work was probably the reason he was let go but it had been a most fortunate situation for Skip. *Now it would be different. Someone new would most likely not allow him the freedom he had now. Someone new would ask questions. How could he continue to hide the experiments that he had going. Could he move them to OMEGA?*

He decided a lunch off the campus of the company was what he needed. He gave Ron a call and they agreed to meet an hour later at the Canoe. Ron arrived after Skip and took his seat in the booth with no grace at all. This wasn't Ron's usual demeanor. He started tapping the table top with his left hand and his eyes darted around the room. After the waitress took their order, Skip asked him

"Okay, so what the hell is wrong with you?"

Ron focused on his lunch partner and asked in a somewhat sarcastic tone "What makes you think there is something the matter?"

"Well, I can see it for myself. What's the matter?"

"I keep getting the unsettling feeling that I am being watched or followed. I can't put my finger on it, but last night I saw a car that I didn't recognize on the street outside my condo. And then this morning, the car, I think it was the same one, was behind me as I went to work. I put a call in last night to my father and I kept hearing clicks on the line. It's starting to creep me out."

"Now exactly why would anybody do this to you?" Skip was annoyed that Ron was sharing this with him. He knew they were both "under the radar" and he wanted it to stay that way.

Ron took a deep breath, arranged his napkin on his lap and then spoke with a bit more control.

"I keep thinking it has something to do with the money I owe. I mean what else could it possibly mean. I got another call from my client and I told him about the meeting in San Diego. I told him you would be meeting with prospective industry reps and that it would happen at that time. He seemed to be placated, I thought. He now wants some kind of time line. He never, ever mentioned this before so he must be getting some kind of pressure too."

Ron took a sip of his beer and added "I now see the benefits of a written contract, nice and legal with due dates and no additional pressures. I will never, ever do this again." Their food arrived and Skip started in on his morning's news.

"Well, here is something that should or could really cause some discomfort. That is, if I was the sort that responded to such stuff. My boss got the notice that he has got six months left to work at the company and he was even offered the option of doing it at home. The stupid idiot is crying like a baby. I would say crying into his milk but of course, I would have to say into his boozed-up coffee!"

Skip took a bite of his sandwich and proceeded with his mouth half full, "I'm not sure what it means for me but I'll figure it out. Right now it is giving me a slightly uneasy feeling. I think I am in good enough stead in the department that I don't have to worry. Most likely, they will find me another boss or let me stay with the new hire."

Ron didn't know what to say. He wasn't familiar with the hierarchy at the company and his enthusiastic backing of the "genius" of his friend never allowed him to think of Skip being in any kind of precarious position there. He had taken it for granted that Skip would stay there until he decided to leave. "What do we do now?"

Skip looked up and in contempt said "Well, I can't image you doing anything at all. Just keep quiet, calm and eat your sandwich, I'll take care of my end of things." Skip changed the subject to sports and they finished their lunch.

When Skip returned to his lab, there was a note on his lab bench. He was to call Marylou in Human Resources immediately. He took a deep breath and dialed the number. He was needed at a meeting in Room 403 in B wing at 4:00pm. He looked at the clock and saw that he had time to feed his cells.

When 3:45pm rolled around, Skip took a notepad and left the lab. *What is this about? It must be about Charlie. Well we will just have to find out.* Skip entered into the Human Resources office and took a seat until the secretary asked him to come into the meeting room. There were three men in the room and Skip knew only one of them. The more formally attired man who seemed to be in charge was sitting directly across from him at the table while the other two men were seated next to each other at one end of the table. The man with the tie introduced himself.

"I am Martin Bell and we have some questions for you." At this point he opened a folder and moved some papers around. "It appears that you have gotten good evals in the past. He seemed to be collecting his thoughts as he spoke. He continued on "as you now know Dr. Simmons has decided to retire and that presents us with some new opportunities." Skip immediately hated the guy. *Retired, my ass, "Fired" is the proper word.*

Skip looked right into the man's eyes, while waiting curiously as to what the question might be. "Mr. Chandler, are you stealing from us?"

Skip's mind drew a blank for a microsecond and then his breathing started to be a little deeper.

"What do you mean?" he asked while his mind reconnected and he started to reel though all possibilities. He had never ever been questioned on any of the orders he had placed. He had never been searched when he left the buildings and he had been very careful. He had never taken anything big like equipment. He had "borrowed" some chemicals and some disposables but how would they or could they trace that to him.

He leaned in and said "Exactly what are you accusing me of?" At this point he looked at one of the men sitting at the table and got the distinct impression that this man was a company lawyer. He had the look. He wasn't a scientist, none of them were. Skip knew the science personnel. The man had opened his briefcase and was shuffling papers around. Skip looked back at Mr. Bell who had noticed Skip's eyes staring at the man seated on his left.

"This is Mr. Knowlton. He represents the company legally and of course you already know Jim Smart, Head of Human Resources."

"And you sir," Skip asked in a slightly irritated voice "who do you represent?"

"It really isn't important at this time to talk about me. Will you please answer the question?"

Skip leaned back in his chair and then repeated "What are you asking me?"

Mr. Bell then put his paper down and started in "Well you see here is the problem. In the last month, we have gone to your lab three times and you have been nowhere to be found. We have evaluated your lab's activity with regards to Dr. Simmons. We would like to know where you were. If you are not in work and we are paying you to be in work then you are stealing from the company."

Skip then took a deep breath and answered tersely, "Well, let's see. If you came looking for me on the third or the tenth, then I wasn't here because I left my house at 6:30am to go to the abattoir to pick up beef brains. You know what an abattoir is, right?"

Skip's tone could best be described as respectfully surly "It's a four hour round trip and then I spent the rest of the day until about 8:00pm in the cold room. You didn't check the cold room when you were looking for me, did you? You know the room I am talking about. It's in the back of the lab and has a ten degree Celsius temperature. It's the one where we have to wear heavy duty gloves and coats to keep warm? Whenever we isolate certain factors, we have to use the fresh bovine brains."

He continued on "Did you look for me in the centrifuge room? I often spend hours there, just isolating sample fractions. I really don't goof off around here because, and this may surprise you, I really like what I do! Did you ask my boss, Dr. Simmons, where I was?"

Skip was on a roll. *These asshole executives don't know a damn thing about what is done here. They could be at some department of god-knows-what, pushing papers all around their desks for all they knew.* He relaxed his body and with a straight face ended with "I really don't know what else to say. I may not be here when you are looking for me, but I come in on Saturdays and work late many nights. I don't get paid "overtime" or whatever they call it in the industrialized world when you put in more hours. I get paid in satisfaction. That is probably hard to understand when you are not directly doing something with your hands or when you are doing something concrete which can actually be rewarding for itself." At this point Skip was starting to overshoot the goal of answering the inquiry. He decided to shut up and sit there.

Mr. Bell looked several times into his briefcase, shuffled papers, and occasionally looked up at Skip. He was clearly unsettled and would never admit to embarrassment before the other present.

"Well, I can see that we need to perhaps change the way we keep track of our employees and we thank you for this enlightening conversation. I guess that is all for the present." Skip was being dismissed but dismissed with his job intact.

# CHAPTER NINETEEN
## SKIP HAS LUNCH WITH THE ORDINARY

**IF THERE WAS A PERSON** who could find and disinter the bones of a body of past malfeasance, then Skip was that man. Skip would look into Mr. Bell and find out exactly who he was. A man who was so presumptuous and condescending would certainly have skeletons in his closet. He was always willing to learn about corporate behavior. After all, he saw himself in the near future having a change of position in the world of biomedical science business. Why would a company as large as *BIOFUTURE* be worried about a lab tech's time?

Skip made his way to the vivarium. Carrying a notebook, he made his way into the area where his animals were being cared for. To his utter amazement, he heard the voice of Phil Jackson, the supervisor of the animal caretakers who worked with the veterinarian. Phil ran a tight operation and kept it in compliance and more importantly immaculately clean. He knew just about as much as the vet regarding small animal diseases. The other voice was that of Mr. Bell. Phil didn't suffer fools lightly and

Mr. Bell was all that. Skip entered into the small autoclave room where the two men were standing.

"Please excuse me but I need to ask some questions of Phil and I just need a quiet moment of time." In the most smarmy voice, he looked at Mr. Bell and said "You don't mind, do you? Just for a minute." Phil excused himself and left Mr. Bell furiously writing in his notebook.

"Phil, this man is a parasite. Do what you can to get rid of him. He is irritating everyone around here except the administration. I don't like him and you shouldn't have to put up with his insulting questions. Please just go along with me and I'll help you get him the hell out of here."

Phil turned to look back at the room with Mr. Bell and then said "Ok. What do you have in mind?"

"Just follow my lead." Skip said as he entered a room filled with animal cages and the ever present Mr. Bell still writing like a mad man. Skip, while ostensibly checking his binder and paperwork, started in.

"Phil, I just wanted to tell you that I am up to date on all my vaccinations. Those rats were really sick. Do they know how that bug got in here? I mean, you guys are so careful. I am very grateful to have had my shots. I didn't realize how often you have to get them. Thanks again for the notice" Phil, being no dope, immediately got the picture. Skip gave a slight smirk as he left the facility.

On the next day, when the clock showed 11:30 am, he picked up his lunch bag and headed for the company's cafeteria. He entered the spacious and airy room filled with a dozen long wooden tables with matching red-seated chairs. One whole wall was filled with floor to ceiling glass windows overlooking the south end of the campus area.

The view was filled with rolling golden hills and trees with yellow and brown leaves. Such was winter in California. Off in the distance, the animal vivarium sat with steel chain link fencing closing it off from the rest of the facility. Skip made his way to a table that had two women already sitting at it.

The two lab techs worked in the pulmonary research unit. Liz was a fifty year old, small wiry woman who had been with the company since it started up. She knew just about everybody and was pretty well liked in return. Sitting with her was Shelly, another story altogether. She was much younger and was considered fairly attractive. Even Skip would give her that. If she could have kept her mouth shut for five minutes without rattling on and on, she would have been even more attractive. She, upon seeing Skip, pushed her hair behind her ear and was hoping that improved her chances with him.

Liz pushed her tray over slightly indicating that Skip should sit next to her. "Well, well, look who's here! What brings you here and out of the lab?"

Skip sat down, opened his lunch bag and pulled out a ham and cheese sandwich. He looked up at the women and asked "I suppose that you have heard about my boss getting canned?" He took a bite of his sandwich and looked out the window. He turned his head back to the two women and waited for them to answer.

"I heard something about it but not anything in detail." said Shelly.

Skip then measured his words and said, "I had a visit with a Mr. Bell and I can't help but think that it has something to do with Clark's firing. It wasn't exactly a firing but rather an 'early retirement'. You know the kind of retirement that you have no choice over."

Shelly then piped up, "I heard about this guy, I think it was him. Someone over in the renal division got into it with a short balding man who gave her a hard time about some orders she placed. She was kind of upset. It probably is the same guy. He was really snippy and didn't give her a chance to really answer the questions."

Skip then threw in some chum for the shark-ladies to chew on. "Well, what else have you heard about him. Is he some kind of efficiency expert. I think it's the same guy, a Mr. Bell."

Just as the three of them were going nowhere with the info on Mr. Bell, a tall, thin and energetic man entered the cafeteria. A quick wave of the hand and he was at their table. Bruce Swift worked in the animal care facility and also was in charge of all the paperwork involved in ordering supplies and paper work in maintaining the facility in compliance with the federal agencies. He moved freely among the lab techs as well as the paper pushers in the offices.

Bruce sat down with a plop and put his tall coffee down. "Well, you know there's this guy floating around here who has managed to irritate a lot of people. His name is 'Mr. Bell' and he is aptly named as in 'ding a ling.' I wonder if he has something to do with Dr. Simmons's situation as well as your grilling, Skip?"

Skip was a little taken aback that Bruce, and therefore others, knew about his interview with the irritating Mr. Bell.

Bruce went on. "You know how we like it down in the vivarium. We're a very happy lot with quiet, little tiny mouse and rat squeaks, the sound of the metal cages going into the wash and the occasional unofficial visits which have been known to occur."

Skip knew that there were such little occasional visits on the part of some of the lab techs who 'ran away from home' for a few minutes with the crew from the vivarium, who were generally a lot less uptight than the lab personnel. He ignored the gossip about trysts behind the tall stacks of animal feed.

Bruce checked his audience to make sure they were still with him. "Well, we got a call that someone was coming down. He knocked loudly to be let in and then proceeded to push us aside. He then proceeded to go from room to room, looking at who knows what: washing rooms, the brood rooms, all of it was open to him. However, he did make the ultimate mistake."

"Mr. Bell got bolder than he should have been. Yessiree, he made the ultimate mistake." At this point Bruce asked his fellow lunch companions, "and what do you think that was?" The women each gave a snicker, looked at each other and then back to Bruce awaiting the answer.

"Well he put his hand on Phil Jackson's arm and told him to bring him to the washing rooms. Now as you probably know, or have heard by way of rumor, no one touches Phil. I mean no one except his wife, his children and maybe his grandchildren, although I am not so sure about them, either."

At this point Shelly couldn't contain herself "What do you mean, 'he doesn't like to be touched?'" Bruce then gave her an impatient look and explained "touched like hugs, shaking hands etc. Some people don't like it. I do not know the why of it. I only know the what of it."

He continued on "Now an ordinary person like me, watching this whole episode, would have noticed that Phil gave him a glare that could have paralyzed or withered the arm that was on his sleeve. Phil slowly released his grasp and walked away which was a good thing. Mr. Bell, not to be ignored then proceeded to follow Phil and pepper him with stupid questions. Having noticed that Phil was an older black man with some kind of uniform or lab coat on, Mr. Bell figured he must be the janitor and not someone of greater consequence. His mistake."

Bruce took a long sip of his coffee and continued on with his audience in rapt attention. "Mr. Bell then started asking a bunch of questions like "what do you do to save on water usage?' and 'what exactly do you do, Mr. Jackson?' Only he didn't say Jackson, he said Johnson. Then he asked the question which sealed his fate, 'why do you have to wash the cages so often? Couldn't you do it every other time instead.' This was clearly too much. I could actually see the muscles in Phil's jaw twitch!"

He didn't exactly want anyone in a suit hearing what came next. "This was the last straw for Phil. When Bell finally came out of one of the rat rooms, Phil came up behind him, grabbed his arms and turned him around to the surprise of the bold Mr. Bell. Phil said with a great deal of concern 'you did get your inoculations, you know, your vaccinations before coming here, right? I mean, we all have our inoculations and vaccinations. We keep a close watch on having our shots right up to date. We just had our shots for tuberculosis and dengue fever, just this past Monday. You know how much trouble animals can be and boy we sure have had some trouble lately. We hardly think of it because we have regular immunizations. You know how the animals are. He repeated slowly and then more slowly and softly 'yes, we have had some problems lately. I've heard the fevers and headaches are the worst and come on really slowly before you get hit full blast with all the other symptoms. This is what I have been told anyways,' and with this he slowly looked away."

Then smoothly as can be, Bruce shook his head and continued on. "Phil is a genius. He looked so sincerely into his face and said 'You went into so many rooms without even reading the warnings. I don't know what you were exposed to. Most of the animals are very healthy. Just a few are really sick' Mr. Bell's face turned a pasty white and his pupils dilated. He took his clipboard and held it more tightly to his chest. Phil took the stunned man's arm and escorted him to the door, opened it, pushed him out and slammed it shut. You know the beauty of it all? A guy like Bell would never ever admit to such a blunder. He'll just suffer in silence waiting for the symptoms to show up. Beautiful, a really beautiful ending to Mr. Bell's adventure." Bruce looked up to see the smiles on the faces of his audience knowing their subtle realization of how a fox could outsmart a weasel.

Skip made fast assessment: Mr. Bell would not be a problem. He decided to up his energy at his own private lab. This place was going to be a drag, come sooner or later. He had better get ready for the future.

# CHAPTER TWENTY
## YVETTE TRIES TO KEEP BUSY

**YVETTE LOOKED OUT THE WINDOW** of her Santa Monica home and saw the rose bushes needed pruning but would just have to wait for a better time. Right now, while sipping her coffee, she sat in deep thought as to what her options were. She could wait out this misadventure, living in a little state of terror, fearful of where living her safe life had taken her. Or she could do something, couldn't she? Her mind raced. *What exactly could she do? She could do what scientists do. Make an educated guess, a hypothesis and test it. She would continue her project of researching the Neuroscience abstracts. She would be methodical. She would ask the right questions in a logical manner. She would call Tom Hall and ask for his input. Yes, at least that would be doing something.*

"Tom, are you available for a few hours to help me out. I'm home and I need your perspective." Tom was in his office on campus but promised that he would be over as soon as he could. He would have the afternoon free to help out.

Yvette sat down at the computer and looked at the searches that she had started and decided to scrap them all and start all over again. When Tom arrived, carrying his computer, Yvette felt a sense of relief and urgency and hurriedly started in.

"I need to be part of this investigation. I just cannot let someone rob me of my career, my lab, my energy and my freedom. I have to be doing something." She was now pacing around the room with an energy which took its root in her anxiety.

"So I want to bounce ideas off you and I really do want your honest feedback. I'm going to try to find the thief at the annual Neuroscience meeting. If it's important enough to kill for, then I think the thief is probably going to present it" Yvette focused on the blank face of her friend.

"It's a crazy idea but it is my current hypothesis." She took out a note pad and put a big number one on the first line.

"Therefore, by elimination, I don't think it was one of his bimbos. I just don't think that young women are that crazy about a single guy today. What do you think of that?"

Tom with a small smile, nodded "yes, that's a good start. I didn't know about a theft. What was stolen?"

Yvette had forgotten that he might not know about the missing vials. "Well, Lili tells me there are missing vials from the liquid nitrogen. The nitrogen level was unusually, I might say perilously low, when she went to check it. She is meticulous. If it was low, it was because someone was in there without taking proper care. In the lab, there was dry ice in the sink but no evidence of Mike doing any work with samples. Plus he wasn't working on the missing samples."

Tom gave a nod of approval "Well those are some points to be dealt with. Go on."

She then put a number two on the sheet and continued

"Well, there was the incident of the flying lady scientist hitting the floor with a big push and now for number three. A very specific set of samples were taken and they just happen to be what Kelley was working on. So what has he got to do with it?"

Tom spoke up, "An accomplice or an unwitting witness, perhaps?"

"Perhaps, and I would like to know where his notebook is. Also I thought you could help me with a directed search through the abstracts for the meeting."

Tom suggested that a search of scientists in Southern California would eliminate a lot of candidates. So that was the first search. Of over 16,000 entries, she got the total down to 3203. This figured right for her as California was right on the cutting edge of the Neurosciences with so many research institutions.

"I'm thinking that "neurons" would be best to eliminate a whole bunch of not relevant material." She entered the term and watched as the number of abstracts got reduced from 3203 down to 152.

"Wow! That sure cut it down. Okay what's next?" Tom looked at the screen of his computer and brought up a list of search terms.

"What about a term that is really specific to the use of these samples. What about glia?" She entered that term and now the search went from 152 entries down to 33. They both scrolled down the search terms.

"You know we can't even call the factors by their names

or code numbers because the thief wouldn't be silly enough to use those terms. Do you think we're being silly too?"

"Well what else can we do right now. I think that the timing of the theft was important. What with the annual meeting coming so soon." Yvette then suggested that there could have been previous thefts and she and the lab would not have known about it.

"Perhaps this thief is working on my factors and is presenting the work. I mean, that is our working premise." She felt a little foolish for even postulating what she was thinking.

"Honestly, I don't know where else to go with this. It's something to do." She almost felt embarrassed that she had asked Tom to come over for such an effort. Her mental image was "needle in the haystack".

Tom took a deep breath "I think it is just as good as any other approach. You don't have access to any forensics stuff nor how to use it. You only got what you got which is a possible explanation of the theft. Let's try one more thing. How about the word 'repair?' Yvette thought this was an excellent choice since that's what the stolen factors were involved in the repair of neurons.

Tom plugged the word in and they now got a total of eight abstracts.

"I can handle eight abstracts. I know this is foolish and there isn't a chance in hell that I am going to learn anything but at least I have the delusion that it is going to be okay and that I am doing something to stop the anxiety."

They then read the eight abstracts and made a list of the times and places of the presentations. She would go to the talks and see what she would see. She knew there were hallmarks of activity for her factors. It would be highly unlikely that the thief could present the data without someone asking for that information. That scientist would be her.

# CHAPTER TWENTY ONE
## BRANDELL GOES TO COLLEGE, AGAIN

**IN THE AFTERNOON AFTER LEARNING** of Rich Kelley's death, Brandell headed over to the young student's apartment. The address was somewhat familiar. It was on a street which had one garden type apartment complex after another, all of them filled with students from the University. He got out of his car and felt a surge of ill-defined and blurry memories. He hadn't been in the area since his college days when he had spent his time in an apartment one street away. It had been a wonderful time for him to be alive. He hadn't joined a fraternity as that wasn't an option for a black man in those early years of equal rights activism on campus. He had felt that he was lucky just to be in college and not subject to the draft to be used as cannon fodder in a useless war.

He approached two young women who stood talking on the grassy lawn in front of the building which had been Kelley's home. One of the women had a baby perched on her hip and the other had a can of soda. As soon as they saw the unknown man, they stopped talking and asked if he was looking for someone. It was a type of neighborhood watch, he figured.

He extended his hand and introduced himself. "I'm Detective Young and I would appreciate any information that you can give me about Rich Kelley."

The air became instantly chilly as one of the woman pointed to the upper apartment adjacent to where they were standing. "That's where he lived and that's all I know about Kelley. We were not in the same academic fields."

"I would appreciate it if either of you could hang around for a few moments. The officers upstairs may want to ask you some specific questions about Mr. Kelley and who his friends might have been." The direct look into their faces must have been intimidating because both women declared simultaneously that they only knew him to say hello to and no more. They hadn't socialized with him. And yes he did have a couple of friends who came around but they hadn't really socialized with him. And wasn't he in the sciences? They were both in the School of Social Work and so didn't come across him on campus.

Two police officers and a woman technician from forensics had already arrived. Brandell entered into the student's apartment and was instantly reminded of his own college days. These were essentially Spartan surroundings but there were some differences with the new generation. While he and his roommate had a TV and were grateful for it, this student lived by himself, had a fancy lap top computer, printer, sound system and some kind of computer game hardware. Brandell spoke with the officers who were processing the scene. His eyes scanned the room and came to rest on what was most probably Kelley's desk, a large platform with the lap top computer sitting on it. Here was the usual assortment of pens and dirty coffee cups, candy wrappers and scraps of paper with notes on them. He looked up on the wall and there hung a photo in a cheap frame. In the picture were three young men sitting with some kayaks.

Brandell mouthed the words "Well, whadda you know? Here's Mr. Ponytail." He instructed the team to bag the photo and finished his tour of the place.

When he returned to the station, he placed a call to the forensic lab. "Jody, we just dropped off a photo from the Kelley apartment and I would appreciate a copy of it as soon as possible. Could I come down and get it now." He was already on his way.

With the copy in hand, he examined it much closer. One of the young men, appeared to be of Asian descent and he sported a tee shirt with lettering on it. Mr. Ponytail's arm was stretched out and grabbing a large overhanging branch. The kayaks were at the water's edge with Kelley sitting in one of them. Hanging down from the branch and partially in Ponytail's hand was another tee shirt. Like the first one, it was dark blue with symbols on it. Perhaps Yvette would know something about the letters. It was a short ride to Santa Monica. He would take a chance that she was home. He was pretty sure she wasn't in the lab.

"Well, it's good to see you if" she hesitated "you're not bringing any more bad news."

"No, that's not it and I only have a moment. I have a picture here and I wanted to know if you recognized either of the two guys in the picture with Kelley." Yvette gave the photo the once over and told him that they were not familiar at all and that she was pretty sure they had never been to the lab.

"I am going to try to determine what's on the Tee shirts, too. Maybe we can get a clue as to the identity of either of the two young men." It wasn't necessary to tell her why he was interested in Ponytail.

She examined the photo and then said slowly "Well, it's some kind of Greek letters. The fabric is folded and it is difficult to make it out." She took the photo and put it on the copier and enlarged it.

"I see a Delta and an Omega but I can't make out what the first letter is." Brandell had an immediate epiphany he kept it to himself. It was one of those moments when something mysterious becomes totally clear. He thanked her, took his photo back and immediately headed out to the University's police department.

Once he had the two names of fraternities with Delta and Omega in their names, he headed on over to the street aptly name "Fraternity Row." On it were nine large Victorian era houses with almost identical personae and which provided housing for the University community's Greeks. Large lawns were well manicured while the wrap around porches held benches and an occasional swing. On the front of each house were the Greek initials which signified the name of the fraternity within. Brandell thought the places looked pretty clean considering the active night life the places must have offered. He had a short list to visit. The first one was Alpha Delta Omega and the second would be Tau Delta Omega. If either of the frat houses had tee shirts to commemorate their illustrious brethren, then he would be in luck.

At Alpha Delta Omega, no one had answered the door but one of the members entering the house held the door open for him. Brandell walked straight in and looked around. The room was a spacious comfortable place full of soft comfy couches and refined arm chairs. A fireplace was at one end of the room while a circular staircase wound around to the second floor at the opposite end. It was all very civilized. It was guaranteed to please and comfort parents who were better off not knowing what drunken bacchanals occurred on the premises. Brandell surmised that the drinking parties and general mayhem were carried on downstairs where parents were less likely to venture.

A young man wearing levis and a grey sweat shirt entered the room from somewhere in the back of the house and stared at Brandell. Tall with dark curly hair and heavy rimmed glasses, he stared at Brandell not quite making out what he was doing here. If his thoughts could be read, they would say "Older Black man. What the hell is he doing here? There's nobody Black here so he couldn't be someone's father? Oh crap, maybe he's the father of that young luscious babe who stayed too long at the last party. She was a mess but we didn't do anything bad to her."

Instead, Brandell heard, "Sir, could I help you? Are you looking for someone?"

Brandell gave an ever so slight smile. "Well exactly. I am most certainly looking for someone but he isn't a member, at least not now. He would have graduated some years ago."

Brandell looked around to see if there were pictures of the fraternity brothers on the wall. There weren't any that were labeled.

"Do you have some kind of archive or record of who was or is still a member of the Fraternity?"

At this point, the young man decided on attitude. *Who was this guy thinking he could just come in and learn about the sacred membership of the fellow brothers.* He calmly headed for the door he started to open, as if to escort Brandell out. With arrogance born from privilege, the young man stated

"We do not give out the names of our brothers, either active or graduated. So sorry."

He wasn't sorry at all and Brandell knew it. He therefore had no other choice but to move his jacket to the side and flash the Detectives gold shield affixed to his waist. While he may have wanted to slap the condescending smirk off the young man's face, this simple display of dominance, gave him equal satisfaction."

"Well, you see son, you may not want to give it to me but I do have the authority to take it from you. I'm Detective Brandell Young and you can help me out here or I can leave, get a warrant and then take over the house while we search for a list of fraternity brothers."

The young man's jaw dropped just slightly and quickly turned into a plastic smile.

"Oh, so sorry detective. I didn't realize who you were."

The young man wasn't quick enough to spontaneously lie so he blurted out "We have a Book of Honor. I'll go get it." He turned quickly on his heels hoping that the detective wouldn't follow him. He gave the room a quick once over before opening a large door.

He looked over his shoulder at the detective and continued "It's in the lounge. It has pictures of all the brothers according to their year. It tells what they were into, what their major was, where they went after graduating. Sometimes it is kept up to date and sometimes not. Just depends on the brother."

He excused himself from the room. Brandell looked again at the room. He walked around and looked at the photos on the wall. So pleasingly civilized. Yet he knew of more than one complaint of wildness ending in violence, date rape, illicit drug use, and riotous behavior erupting onto the lawns in the middle of the night. Brandell's thoughts on this paradox of civility and corruption, was interrupted by the return of the young frat brother who was carrying a large and heavy album.

He placed the book on the coffee table and in his most smarmy voice asked "Do you mind telling me who you are looking for? Or even why?" The bravado was gone and curiosity took its place.

Brandell didn't answer. He opened the tome and started in the back, looking at the past graduates. The young man, trying to appear not-overly concerned, offered that his name was Stuart Rodell. He was President of the local chapter of the national fraternity, and was known to his frat brothers by his nickname, "the King". He would be glad to help out. Even more so if he knew what the Detective was looking for.

Brandell took out the photo and showed it to Stuart, who fingered the photo and then opened the book looking for members who had graduated in recent years. "Here we go. I think this is one of the guys." Stuart's finger was positioned over the picture of a young man of Asian descent whose name was Ron Hattori.

"Yes, he was a business major and now works in an

investment company. Local boy, West LA." Brandell took down what was entered as the most recent address. The young man looked somewhat relieved that this intruder would soon leave. He reached for the album but was quickly rebuffed by the icy stare of the detective.

Brandell now sat in the largest of the leather chairs and slowly turned the pages several more times. In a matter of minutes, he came to Richard "Iceman" Kelley. He read his biography: Biology major, heading to graduate school, likes the outdoors, kayaking, ice climbing and mountain biking. Brandell didn't need his address. This he had under his belt. Brandell flipped through the remainder of the album. He was now into the students who had graduated four years before Kelley. He turned the page and there he was. Smirking, good looking, flashing a great set of teeth, and long blond hair.

Mr. Pony Tail now had a name, Harrison "Skip" Chandler. He was a biology major with a business minor. Brandell read the kid's personal statement "I'm going into research and will eventually start my own biotech company." Brandell's face showed an almost imperceptible smile which indicated his immense pleasure at finding this guy. He wasn't all that concerned that the arrogant little prick standing before him would make a few phone calls after he left. A fraternity brother had a right to know if someone was looking for him. Otherwise, how could he decide to not be found.

# CHAPTER TWENTY TWO
## FINDING SKIP

**HE HAD A WORK ADDRESS** for Hattori but not for Chandler. He made his way to West Los Angeles and started looking at the addresses of the tall office buildings lining Wilshire Boulevard. After he parked in the large lot adjacent to Rising Sun Landmark Investments, he made his way into the lobby where a petite receptionist connected him to Ron Hattori's office. Behind her pleasant face, was curiosity. Brandell could always detect this sense of interest in those whom he came in contact with peripherally during his day in the field. What did a detective want here? She opened Ron's door, stepped back and perhaps looked just a bit too long at the detective as he entered into the room.

Ron raised himself slightly in his chair and extended his hand. Keeping his cool, he asked, "So how can I help you?"

Brandell produced the picture of the three frat brothers and said "As you probably know, Mr. Kelley is dead, poisoned in fact." In spite of his every effort to appear calm, a slight sheen of perspiration was forming on Ron's forehead.

"I didn't know that." He wasn't lying. Work had kept him pretty busy lately and he hadn't read the paper for several days. Furthermore, Skip had said nothing about this when they were at lunch. "When did this happen? Do you know why?"

Brandell gave him the outline of finding Rich outside the restaurant and the subsequent failure of the young student to survive his misadventure. "How do you know he was murdered? I mean couldn't he have eaten something bad?"

Ron's outer appearance of calm belied the intense panicked thinking inside his head where questions about his death and Skip Chandler's involvement were like bricks in a crumbling wall, falling quicker than could be dealt with.

"Tell me about Rich's friends. Did you socialize with him regularly?" Ron quickly answered that they only met occasionally, that they were fraternity brothers and that other than their interest in outside sporting adventures, they didn't really hang out so much.

"Can you tell me about the other young man in the photo?" Brandell didn't hit him with this right away even though Skip Chandler was his reason for being here.

"Well, that is Skip Chandler, another fraternity brother. I don't think that he socialized with Rich all that much either. He works at BIOSCIENCE. You know the big biotech company in Thousand Oaks. He keeps pretty busy out there." Ron was carefully choosing his words, trying to say anything that would deflect attention away from Skip.

"Do you know what he does out there?"

Ron answered with an air of detachment, "Oh, he's just a lab tech out there. Been there since he graduated from the university. I don't know much about his work. We don't really talk that much about it."

"I thought you said you didn't get together?" Time to apply a little pressure thought the detective.

"Well, we don't, really. But when we do it for outside stuff not work related, we're in very different kinds of work." Ron was trying to keep a disinterested demeanor while inside he was churning. *What had Skip done now? Did he do this?* Of course this line of thinking would lead him to the inevitable, *When will it be my turn to be dealt with?*

Brandell pressed on with more questions about the fraternity brothers activities but he had gotten what he needed. If they could not find Pony Tail at home, which seemed to be the case after repeated attempts by his uniformed colleagues, then he would go to BIOFUTURE.

"Well thank you and if you can think of anything about Mr. Kelley that would help us, please let me know" and with this, Brandell handed the young man his card.

The next morning, Brandell made the drive to Thousand Oaks, a peaceful ride as the freeway rolled along into the suburban area. He found himself entering into the main building and was asked to wait until Dr. Clark Simmons came into the big lobby. After the two men exchanged introductions, they went back to the secured laboratory area. Brandell noticed that Clark had a slight tremor and appeared to have a rather unimpressive affect.

"Oh, Skip isn't here today and in fact, he asked for a few days off. He is going to be at the Neuroscience meeting coming up however. I haven't a clue where he is today. We have our poster talk already to go so I thought it was okay for him to take a few days off.'

Brandell's eyes were canvassing the entire lab space outside Dr. Simmon's office. "So what is he working on here?" The lab space was huge and filled with expensive equipment. Brandell kept up the small talk and finally got to the main point of coming here. "Do you have toxins here that are dangerous?"

Clark started to wear a slight smile but quickly changed realizing he was talking to a detective. "Well of course we do. Many of the reagents and biologicals we use are very dangerous if you got them on your hands or ate them. We all know that and we warn the unsuspecting."

Brandell then made his main move, "If I were to ask you if I could have a specific poison, would you let me take it to have it analyzed in our lab? I am talking about tetrodotoxin specifically."

Clark was a bit taken off guard. "Tetrodotoxin? Sure we have it here. I think it's in the locked cabinet in the lab. We haven't used it in years. There are better agents out there now." He went over to the cabinet, unlocked it and removed a small bottle. "Why do you want this?"

"We're looking into sources of the material in the area. It's for a police investigation involving a poisoning. We'd like to get a profile of what it looks like in our labs." All of what he said was true. He didn't need a warrant if it was freely given and furthermore, it didn't belong to Skip. So there was no problem there. He placed the tiny bottle into a sealed evidence bag and documented it.

"What has this to do with Skip Chandler? Is he involved

in something creepy? Because I would believe it if he were."
Brandell simply told him he couldn't comment.

Clark continued on, "That kid has something going on. I can just feel it. I'm retiring soon so I really don't care anymore. You might be interested in this." At this point Clark reached across his desk and pulled out a sheet of paper which was an invoice. "I didn't order this. I didn't authorize it and we have no record of it here in the lab. What is of interest to me is the address where the materials were sent. I found this in a bunch of papers with other invoices. The address, Tech Drive, is in a biomedical industrial park, right here in Thousand Oaks. I have never heard of Omega Scientific. There is no name associated with it." Perhaps this is of interest to you. Brandell figured he got more than he bargained for. He would visit Omega Scientific since he was right here in town.

The small research area was filled with small spaces filled with various supply companies and startup companies of various ilk. He found the space for Omega Scientific and found it quiet.

# CHAPTER TWENTY THREE
## NEUROSCIENCE IN A BIG SPACE

**YVETTE SPENT THE WEEKEND PREPARING** for her attendance at the Neuroscience meeting. She herself was presenting her lab's work on Monday morning at 11:00am while her student's presentations were scattered throughout the week. For that she was grateful. She would get her own presentation out of the way so that she was free for the remainder of the week to visit poster talks, meet old friends, check up on her students' presentations and look at all the displays of new books and equipment. She had prepared her students over the weekend for their talks and she was looking forward to this most unusual "vacation" from the lab.

She had no doubt that some of her colleagues knew about the murder of one student but probably didn't know about the death of the second. How was she going to handle this? Well, she would tell them they knew as much as she did, which was limited and change the subject. If that didn't work to divert the conversation, she would excuse herself to go to a specific talk she just couldn't miss. It would be okay. She left her home fully expecting the trip into the convention center to be more than an hour. She practiced her presentation in her head and was satisfied that it was okay.

The air was electric. The Grand Concourse was filled in its center with row after row of vendors of all kinds. There were so many different kinds of equipment to check out, books to flip through, free samples to take and so many faces to recognize. Yvette picked up her name tag from the ID center at the entrance and entered the arena. Three steps into the giant hall and she recognized a colleague from across the country, a fellow neuroscientist from MIT. Her greeting and smile came from her heart as she grabbed the out stretched hand of an old friend and researcher at the NIH.

"Yvette, I am so glad to see you here. I was afraid that you had gone into hiding! It sounds so dreadful."

Yvette now knew that every interaction with her fellow scientists at the meeting would be tainted by their curiosity and concern.

"Well, I am here to forget just for a few days the awfulness of what has happened. It is all under investigation so we don't know a damn thing about any of it. The kid was a philanderer. We do know that." She wasn't about to tell them anymore. They didn't need to know anymore! "We'll see how it all works out." She would change the subject.

"I read your paper in *NEUROSCIENCE*. That was an extension of the work you presented in Houston, right? Very elegant. I am presenting in a few hours in the Holmby Room, 11:00am."

She looked at her watch. "I should be heading over

there. Can we get together for lunch after?" Her colleague agreed and they set up a meeting place. She smiled and headed off to the meeting room. On the way, she greeted three more colleagues with a smile, a wave of the hand and a quick dismissal.

"Giving my talk in a few minutes. See you later." She entered the room from the darkened back area, took a seat and quietly waited for her introduction. She had done it dozens of times before and knew the drill.

Later in the afternoon, she took out her little list of eight "presentations of interest". One, number 206, was a poster talk at 2:30pm. She made her way over to the presentation and stopped several posters ahead of number 206. She thought the presenter looked familiar. Yes, she was a graduate student of Lawson Clark over at the VA hospital's Neuroscience lab. Small and fragile looking, Yvette quickly dismissed her as not the hammer-wielding type. She read her poster information and listened as the shy student answered questions by the passing students and scientist interested in cell growth and repair. She was competent but way to inexperienced to be looking viciously for factors to steal. She was probably in her first year of school. Yvette engaged the student trying to lead her to tell everything with grace and confidence. No, this one wasn't THE one.

Yvette moved on down the line to the second presentation, number 289 on her list. She did not know the presenter even though he was from the area. His poster had marvelous electron micrographs of cells making contact with each and they were artfully done. He had the sophistication to understand what her factors could do but this student's work wasn't even close to what she was doing. She dismissed him as a candidate for "murderer" as well. She felt relieved that her little private game of "catch the culprit" wasn't being successful. After all what would she do if she did get that funny feeling that she was in the presence of the very one who had killed in her lab.

She spent the rest of the afternoon looking at exhibits and chatting with old friends. She had not run into any students and she was glad for that too.

On Tuesday morning, Yvette was looking forward to a day of intense science. Oral presentations in the morning and after lunch, the posters would be the next thing on her agenda. The posters were always interesting in that one could never predict what one would see. While some posters were expertly prepared with little new information contributed to the world of science, others could look like they were scratched together the night before and yet gave wonderful data. Lost in a world of cells, neurons, neurotoxic drugs and seemingly endless interesting topics, Yvette made her way down the long line. When she reached the end of the first row, she decided to keep going around the corner to see a few more posters, and then break for coffee.

She looked up and was stopped in her tracks. There before her stood Brandell Young, notepad in hand and wearing a name tag. She walked up to him and looked to see what his eyes were fixed on. The poster was entitled "Cell Repair with Harlophen." She read the authors' names and saw that they were from one of the many big research companies in the Thousand Oaks area. Neither name rang a bell. No, she didn't recognize them at all.

"So are you planning on a change in careers?" She asked

as she sidled up to the detective. He turned and gave her a subdued smile, place a subtle finger to his lip and gave a nod of acknowledgment. He was listening very carefully to the man speaking. When the time was over for this particular talk, the author picked up his briefcase and walked away. Brandell turned to Yvette and suggested that they move to a less dense area, get some coffee and talk.

"Well we have made some progress in the case and it has brought me here." Brandell reached for the coffee creamer and looked around at the table where they sat. There was no one else around.

"It seems that Mr. Kelley had lunch with a young man before he showed up poisoned. This fellow is a lab tech at *BIOFUTURE*. Most importantly, we can't seem to find him. He hasn't shown up at work for several days. He was supposed to give this talk but his boss did the poster without him. He doesn't know where the fellow is either. "Brandell's eyes never stopped panning the faces of others passing by large open space around them.

"You may not know it but we went to visit Mr. Skip Chandler at his work place. Surprise, they had some tetrodotoxin in the lab and we sent it out for analysis. It matched the characteristics of what was found in Rich Kelley's body. By the way, your tetrodotoxin did not. In any case, we're looking for Mr. Chandler, or as I refer to him, Pony Tail."

She gave a quizzical look and he immediately answered "Distinguished by his long blond hair worn pulled back into a pony tail."

She asked for a picture of the guy. "No. Maybe I recognize him. I'm not sure."

"I am scanning all the talks and hanging out for a couple of days in case he shows up. His boss says he is a very serious sort of scary lab tech who envisions himself as an entrepreneur. In other words, the kid has plans."

Yvette then made a quick decision and brought out her list of special talks she needed to visit. "Well, I can't stand it any longer. Not knowing what is going on in the lab or out of the lab. It's making me crazy. I decided to do a little investigation myself and please don't laugh. I looked at the collection of presentations at the meeting and as you know sitting here and looking around, there are thousands of them. I did a computer search of all the talks originating from the Southern California area. Then, I eliminated from those hundred, the one which have nothing to do with what I am into. Things like neurophysiology and neuropsychology. The list got shorter. Finally after spending some time with a colleague who wanted to be in on the chase, we came up with the short list here." At this point, she held out the list of eight presentations.

"I went to the first two. Neither one looked promising and neither one of them had a blond ponytail.

Brandell's eyes went over the list and registered nothing out of the ordinary until he reached the second to the last presentation. He took his pen and underlined the name

"Do you know this person?" Yvette's eyebrows furrowed and she shook her head. The detective's eyes were still scanning the large hall. Then turning to Yvette said

"Well 'Harrison Chandler' and 'C. Harrison' makes me look twice. Do you know anything about this company, Omega Scientific? When is this talk?" he asked.

Yvette checked the list again. "Tomorrow at 10:30am.

It's over on the other side of the hall, one of the larger rooms, the Pantage Room. Maybe they are anticipating a crowd. I mean the title is very inviting, "The Role of New Growth Factors in Spinal Cord Injury." I mean, it has it all!"

Brandell took out his phone and searched for Omega Scientific. It didn't show up. That was odd, he thought. Let's visit Mr. Harrison's talk tomorrow, together. In the meantime, I am going to continue walking around this place. This is so fascinating and so huge. I never knew there were so many scientists coming to conventions.

"Oh yes, yes, your tax dollars at work." She gave him a quick smile and they parted.

# CHAPTER TWENTY FOUR
## C. HARRISON'S BIG DAY

**SKIP'S DAY WOULD BE PERFECT.** It had to be. He had contacted his "interested parties" to tell them where to be and what to expect. Their presence would go unnoticed in the larger audience but in his mind, it meant that they would be there for the first public demonstration of his work. They certainly would see him answer any and all questions with the confidence he would exude. He would give them hints as to the financial implications of investment in his work. They would more importantly, trust him. Of this he was certain and this was most critical. Their trust would go a long way to smooth over any little nagging doubts or questions about details.

All he needed was one, just one of the men to take in what he had privately told them and present it at their company's private strategy meetings. Just one and the rest of them could try to raise the ante!

Skip waited in the back of the large hall surveying the audience. He wasn't that outstanding to anyone looking around. Just an ordinary scientist with his briefcase in hand.

He was in the "uniform" of the hip scientist, Levi's and a blue cotton sweater. He had dyed his hair brown and with bitterness, cut his pony tail off. Blond was too frivolous, he thought. He didn't want to be seen as a lightweight. As the clock ticked away, and in between each talk, he moved slowly towards the front of the room. He was waiting for his fifteen minutes. If everyone deserves fifteen minutes of fame, as Andy Warhol said, well, this would be his.

Brandell and Yvette arrived at 8:30am just as the meeting session was starting. Brandell had already informed the security team in this area of the convention center. They knew what he wanted them to do, if he gave the signal. They scanned the room looking for Pony Tail. It wouldn't be likely that he would be there. He just might though. They would wait patiently. They didn't know for sure that Pony Tail was C. Harrison. Although Brandell didn't like that kind of coincidence in the names. Harrison Chandler and C. Harrison just didn't seem right. He didn't like coincidences. If he had to place a bet, he would place it on C. Harrison as his man.

Skip's presentation was scheduled to be immediately after the 15 minute break. He made his way up to the front of the large meeting room while others in the room ran out to refresh their coffees, stand up to stretch and/or leave as new attendees entered the room. While waiting, he walked across the stage and placed his papers containing his meticulously prepared talk on the top of the old wooden podium. He would take this brief break to relax himself in preparation. He lifted his head to survey the room and he started scanning the back rows of chairs. He knew some of the people already assembled and now he was looking for his contacts. The moderator was fiddling with the microphone at his table and greeted him even though it wasn't the official starting time.

"Well Dr. Harrison, we'll need a few more minutes before you start." The room was starting to settle down and fill in. Skip looked at his notes and like a winning race horse at the starting gate, was anxious to be let loose.

It was at this precise moment that he looked at those sitting directly in front of him in the first row. *What the hell is HE doing here? Who is that with him? Why is he sitting there with that strange look on his face?* He wasn't supposed to be here at all. This was unnerving. All he could ask himself is "why" and "what did it mean." He noticed he was holding his breath and he forced himself to inhale deeply. His breathing rate was starting to get accelerated. His stomach was starting to actually make him aware of tension. He kept looking at the front row and mouthed the words

"Why are you here?" He knew that his words wouldn't actually reach the front row, not without the microphone turned on. Could he risk that? He pushed the paper work of his talk to the side and looked for the audio switch. He flipped it and then staring at the front row articulated in a low but distinct voice,

"Why are you here?" Others in the audience dismissed the muffled low voice asking the "philosophical question" as a sound check.

The man in the audience couldn't answer. Ron Hattori was sandwiched between two large Asian men, all three of them were dressed in dark suits and ties. His face upon closer inspection had the look of someone terrorized or at least immobilized. He couldn't or wouldn't answer. Skip asked again with his voice a little higher up the octave scale, a little bit more insistent and now was beginning to be noticed.

"Exactly why are you here? This is a distraction. You have no business here." With this last statement, the crowd started to calm down considerably and started to pay attention. Skip was moving the papers around on the dais and glaring out at his friend and partner. His hands were starting to move over the top of the rostrum. His mind raced with the unanswered question. Why was Ron here at a scientific meeting? He wasn't a scientist. He was in charge of one singular thing he managed to do, but not sufficiently in Skip's mind. Raise the funds to supply the lab. That was it. Ron had been told to stay away under all circumstances, away from any situation which would bring attention to Skip and his work. *Hadn't that been made abundantly clear? No one was to know of their association. No one. He wasn't needed for the scientific aspects of their venture. Why, why, why?*

Sitting at the other end of the front row were Yvette and Brandell. Yvette thought what was happening on the stage a bit out of the ordinary. People did get nervous and start fiddling about. However, they didn't usually start addressing people in the audience before their talk even began, at least not with hostility. That was usually reserved for the question and answer period when long standing rivals questioned the work being presented. On the whole, her fellow scientists were a polite crowd.

Brandell felt the vibration of his cell phone and took the call. One of the other members of his team was calling from the lab space of Omega Scientific. "We just went into the lab space and found something I wanted you to be on to. A few long blond hairs on the floor and hair dye splashed around the sink. Your boy has cut his hair and dyed it too. Thought you might need to know if you are looking for him. We're searching for the vials you mentioned. I'll let you know what's what in a bit."

Yvette leaned over and whispered "I think this is a little bit weird. This guy has a crappy dye job and no pony tail hanging down his back. And who the hell is he talking to?"

Brandell gave the slight hint of a smile and leaned over to her. "Our boy is traveling incognito. New hair job and no pony tail."

While looking over to Yvette, he had a stunning moment of recognition. There sitting just a few seats away, bundled between two noticeably muscular men, was the third man in the photo, Ron Hattori. This was just too much. Coincidences like this are not coincidences at all. They are part of the bigger picture. Brandell's curiosity was piqued. What was the significance of this fellow giving the talk here and now? He decided to wait just a few moments to see what unfolded. He certainly had a more than a few questions for Mr. Chandler.

At just that moment, the moderator welcomed the audience, looked at Skip, and announced, "We now have the talk entitled "The Role of Combination of New Growth Factors in Spinal Cord Injury and Repair." by Doctor C. Harrison of Omega Scientific.

Skip reached for the podium with both hands. He was experiencing a new feeling which wasn't pleasant. Anxiety was grabbing him in his stomach and in his throat. The science was a piece of cake but why Ron was here was befuddling. He could feel his face flush and tried to calm himself. *So what if Ron is here. There's probably a very good reason and I'll ask him after this talk is over. He better get the hell out of here before I meet with my associates.*

Skip looked up at the audience, tried to start talking but all he could see was the two giant men flanking Ron, who was no small guy himself. They had strategically placed themselves directly in his line of sight. Either they wanted a good seat or they were just letting him know they were here to bear witness. They had no expressions on their faces, just dead staring eyes focused on him. He could have sworn that one of them was actually holding on to Ron's lower arm as it rested in his lap.

Skip's body started its own movement, swaying just a little. He couldn't get started. His tongue felt dry and huge in his mouth. His heart had now picked up the sense of fright which was enveloping him. His chest was pounding. His hands clutched the edge of the wooden rostrum. He couldn't remember his starting line. This was his big chance and he was on the verge of screwing it up in a major way. He had to get a hold of himself. He took a deep breath and tried to talk but nothing came out. *Get a hold of yourself, get a hold of yourself. He can explain later. They don't want to hurt you. You don't even know why they are here.*

Skip's internal panic was given a prod by the moderator who told him to proceed with the presentation as the clock was ticking away his time. Just as he was about to speak, his papers fell to the floor in a flurry, spreading out in a tangled mass. He picked them up, not in order of course, and tried to regain his composure. Now he saw a tall black man approaching the side stairs which connected to the stage. *What did he want?* He glanced across the stage to the moderator's chair only to see a uniformed security man coming up the stairs on the far opposite side. They were heading towards him. *What the hell is going on? This is my chance! What is happening here?* Skip's hands took on an agitated life of their own, squeezing the papers and moving them up and down. He couldn't help himself.

Just as Brandell was at the top of the stairs, Skip's hands through no willful movement of their own, slammed down on a button in the back surface of the rostrum. The button was left over from other times when it was necessary to have dramatic entrances and exits for theatrical presentations, which was certainly not what was needed here. The podium with Skip, his notes, his panic and his glossy eyes, started to descend into the sub-floor of the stage. Skip look bewildered as he caught sight of Ron. The two escorts had stood up and were leaving their seats. Ron was between them as they walked most deliberately up the aisles. Ron looked around with a pleading look. Skip and the rostrum were descending slowly and Brandell reached out and grabbed the lanky and befuddled man before his descent into the netherworld was finished. He handed him over to the detective and they left the stage .The audience was abuzz with more noise than the greatest talk had ever generated.

# CHAPTER TWENTY FIVE
## A DIFFERENT PRESENTATION

**BRANDELL INTRODUCED YVETTE TO HIS** fellow detectives as they made their way to the interrogation room. He had secured permission for her to be there behind a one way mirror and she was to have the distinct privilege of observing him question Mr. Chandler. Having her nearby should any science topics come up, was a reassurance for him. Yvette sat quietly in her chair but her eyes were scanning the whole scene. This was a serious business, a way of exploring information that was very different from her daily endeavors. Brandell entered the simple room where Skip Chandler sat. He kept his eyes fixated on the young man. He sat down, folded his arms and just stared.

"We have all the evidence we need to nail you for the murder of Mike Desfleur. Did you know that was his name? The only thing left is to decide what kind of crime it was? Did you plan to kill him? That's the worst case scenario. Life imprisonment under fairly nasty circumstances. Did you kill him in the heat of the moment? That's bad but perhaps not exactly life imprisonment. You're a young man so perhaps getting out when you're sixty years old is better than languishing in prison forever. Were you overcome with anger and killed him because you can't control yourself. You know, became enraged and temporarily insane. That will get you a lot of time in an institution. So we have some choices here. Let's just decide how bad it is."

Skip Chandler stared right back and simply said "I want my lawyer."

At this point, the detective raised his hand and said "call him, we have all day."

Brandell left the room and got himself a cup of coffee. He entered into the back room where Yvette sat and simply stared through the mirror. Skip sat with his cell phone and talked with the lack of affect he demonstrated when he was attempting complete control of any situation. Yvette wanted desperately to question the detective but she didn't dare. Brandell was in some kind of "zone" and she didn't want to be asked to leave. So she sat there, engrossed in the drama as it unfolded. He looked at her and quietly said "we have him, don't worry. We've got him."

He returned to the room where Skip sat and resumed sitting in his chair. "Well, let's see what we can chat about that doesn't require your lawyer present. What kind of work do you do at BIOFUTURE? Are you some kind of helper there? I mean do you assist the scientists in charge, those who do the research?" Brandell was going to rattle this snake. He knew the type, sociopaths who think they are smarter than everyone else in the room but who always have an Achilles' heel. He thought he had Skip's down.

He continued on before Skip could answer "You

probably have to do exactly as they ask you to, following all their directions. I guess lab technicians are just an extra pair of hands for the real scientists." He noticed the color in Skip's face was getting deeper and his jaw was more tightly clenched. Just a little bit more prodding was needed to get the kid going.

"I met your boss. He's a piece of work. How does he even function in the lab? Do you have to cover for him and make him look good? I'll bet he gets all the credit and you just get a paycheck."

Skip could take it no more. "He's an asshole and yes, I do cover for him."

Brandell prodded "Well, how does it work? Do you think up the experiments or just do as he says, if you can even understand him through the booze? How does a young man like yourself, someone smart, get ahead in an environment like that? How do you make your mark?"

Skip couldn't just sit there and take it. He was, in his own opinion, smarter than Clark Simmons on any day of the week. *This guy doesn't know who he's dealing with. This plan has been in motion for months. Every detail has been considered and is under control. I know that the cells are responding exactly the way I anticipated...and that is going to make me famous and rich. What is the life of some busybody graduate student, when the cure for nerve injury is on the other balance of the scale? Probably nothing.*

The door to the room opened and a short, muscular, well-dressed man entered into the room. He offered his hand to Brandell, introducing himself. "I'm Jonathan Post, the lawyer for the Chandler family." Not Skip's lawyer but the family retainer. He's probably had other exposure to the young man's behavior. Brandell got the distinct impression that Jonathan Post would rather have been defending Charles Manson than Skip Chandler. "I am of course going to ask my client to be cooperative since I'm sure he is innocent. What exactly is it that you are charging him with?"

"Well Skip here broke into a research lab at the University and stole some vials. In the process of doing so, he killed a student. We have him on this, so there is no getting out of it. The question is, of course, 'why' and how did it happen? We're not sure if the student was someone he meant to meet there. Perhaps the young man, Mike Desfleur, was helping Skip. You know, telling him about the contents of the vial, perhaps telling him how to use it. You know directing Skip on the proper use of the contents."

Brandell was going to send this psychopath into orbit if it was the last thing he did in the day. "You know Mr. Post, Skip works as a lab tech at *BIOFUTURE*. He feeds the cells and handles the animals. He's not the scientist in charge, although, of course, he probably could have been under different circumstances. By the way Skip, exactly why didn't you go on to get your Ph.D.? You could have done this work and gotten all the credit?"

Skip was circling around the bait and finally couldn't resist. "I had some difficulties with the pea-brained mentor I chose and I left in disgust. I had different plans and now I am working on them. You don't need a Ph.D. to do research." He was still glaring at Brandell who sat quietly with an ever so slight smile. This was going very nicely, he thought.

"What possibly could you do at *BIOFUTURE*? You

have absolutely no status there. Who is going to listen to you? No one!. And now Dr. Simmons is leaving, so you'll probably be transferred to some other lab where they will stick you in some project just to keep you on the payroll, at least temporarily, before they let you go." Brandell would show no mercy.

Mr.Post's hand reached out to Skip's shoulder to remind the young man to keep quiet. But why would Skip keep quiet when a no-nothing detective was all wrong in his assessment of Skip's worth.

"I have worked out something that is going to change the way we think of nerve injury. You wait and see. And remember that you tried to humiliate me here. I won't forget it."

Mr. Post then interrupted. "What exactly do you have to support a murder charge for Mr. Chandler? Let's get on with it or let us leave."

At this point, the door opened and a tall, conservatively dressed woman in a dark blue suit with a folder in her hand entered the room. Mr. Post recognized her immediately.

"I am Angela Witt from the District Attorney's office and I am here to discuss the possibilities of charges with Mr. Chandler. We are going to prosecute you for murder and we are going to win. As of this moment, I am here to listen. If you want some kind of deal, now is the time to cooperate. You had better answer the detective's questions, or take the full brunt of the prosecution's efforts."

Skip had a sneer on his face, but Mr. Post was more interested. "Would you please tell us what you have that convinces you of Mr. Chandler's guilt?" Skip's gaze was focused on the outside activities of the squad room. He had been strategically placed so that he could see who was being brought into an adjacent room for questioning.

Brandell then spoke deliberately and quietly. "Can you tell us how the key to Dr. Bilodeau's lab was in your possession, Skip? We found it in your apartment. Can you explain how your fingerprint found its way onto the liquid nitrogen tank in the laboratory? Can you explain how three vials from Dr. Yvette Bilodeau's lab were found in your private little enterprise called Omega Science? Three little vials which were stolen the night of the murder of Mr. DesFleur?"

While his ears may have been taking in the list of questions from the detective, Skip froze as he saw two detectives bring an unsmiling and somewhat battered Ron Hattori through the room with its collection of desks and into an adjacent interrogation room. Brandell had planned it exactly this way and had instructed the detectives to make sure that Ron spent a few moments out in the general office area. He wanted Skip to know his silent partner was silent no more. Skip became terrified and stood up in defiance. *What was that little weasel going to say? Why did I tell him about the lab? I should have never told him about the mess in the lab. Alright Ron, sink or swim. You didn't tell anybody about it. You're guilty too.*

At this point, he decided to talk. The sneer was gone and in its place, was the face of the negotiator. "Alright, I want a deal. It was definitely an accident."

Brandell gave a sigh which only slightly gave away his inner disgust. He couldn't wait to see how a bludgeoning could become an accident!

"I went to the lab with Rich Kelley's key. I knew what

was in his notebooks and I wanted the samples that he was working on. He wouldn't give them to me, so I decided to go get them myself."

Brandell asked "Did Rich Kelley know what you were doing?"

Skip didn't answer but continued on. "I had the samples in my own ice bucket. I was ready to leave when this snotty graduate student showed up and started giving me a hard time. Then he tried to hit me with that hammer. I defended myself."

Brandell countered with "Details, details, please?" The lawyer seemed relieved and let his client handle the mess he got himself into. Skip recounted the whole grandiose scheme. He collected his materials and got his cells to grow, to reconnect and then he got them to do the same in living animals. He was ready to sell his approach to the first investor to come along. He had them waiting to hear about his progress. And yes, he had done it by himself. Well sort of. He made sure to include his former friend, Ron, in the mix. Skip wasn't going to suffer an indignity by himself. When he finished describing the death of Mike and the theft, he waited for the DA to come in with her decision.

"Well, we won't push for a life term since it sounds like an aggravated situation. We will go for 25 years with no parole for the death of Mr. DesFleur. That's it. No more, no less. Do we have an understanding? Otherwise, I can guarantee you a trial and a life sentence."

Skip gave his attorney a look which said "So what do you think?" And with a slight nod, the deal was done. "I would like to be in a 'position' where there is a decent library." This was his sole request.

At this point, he started to get up thinking that the whole ordeal was now finished. He had implicated Ron and that was satisfying. He would appeal and appeal until the cows came home.

Brandell raised a hand. "Just a moment, we're not through here. You just settled for the death of Mike DesFleur and I can accept what the DA has offered. Twenty five years will keep you busy for a long time. However, we have another issue on the table."

Skip looked at his lawyer and with contempt said "And what more do you want from me?"

"We have another death, another equally gruesome and pitiful death. What about your friend, your frat brother, Rich Kelley. His death is NOT part of the deal we just made. In fact, there is no deal for your part in that. We have all that we need for a conviction for that one too." Skip just stared ahead. All he could think of was his former fraternity brother pleading with him to stop, pleading with him to tell what happened. Skip had been afraid that Rich was a weak link that had to be silenced.

"Do you know in that big brain of yours, that the little bottle of tetrodotoxin we recovered from your lab was from a very old preparation of the drug. According to the paperwork for it from *BIOFUTURE,* it was over twenty years old. It has a few contaminants in it that more recent preps have managed to eliminate. It was good for us because we could identify the drug in Rich Kelley's tissues based on the contaminants. Plus you left the bottle you stole from work in your new lab space. You were the last one to see Rich alive at the Japanese restaurant. They have identified you without a doubt. This second murder seals the deal. You will never see your lab again. You will rot in jail and you will not be doing any more research." At this point, Skip's anger burst through his facade of disengagement.

"You absolutely must let me finish with my cells, I must put them into the deep freeze. You can't just let the cells die. They could change medicine. I must see my cells. It would be a crime to let them die." The police officer took his arms and placed restraints on them. As he was being led away, he was enraged, yelling and protesting loudly about his cells.

Brandell had nothing but contempt for him.

"You will not see any cells again. In fact the only cell which you'll see is the one you will be living in."

# EPILOGUE

**YVETTE AND HER STUDENTS SETTLED** into the new lab. The luxury of sufficient space and the ability to spread out lab equipment was a small consolation. The loss of the two students left a large empty place in their lives. Being scientists now in the age of profit driven motivation before honesty, had given them a particularly painful lesson. There was science and then there was greed-driven and criminal activity using science. The young man who killed their friends was a crazy megalomaniac but he also loved the same pursuit that they did, the advancement of knowledge of life's processes. They would keep that in mind as they went on in their lives as scientific investigators exploring what it means to be human at the cellular level.

Brandell had found the case gripping and very interesting. He now had a new appreciation for all that he did not know about the workings of a science lab. He was happy it was over but found that he liked the professor. Maybe coffee together in the future.

Skip paces in his new home. He knows he was right

and those stupid guys he dismissed were in the way. It was right to get rid of them, they were impeding the progress towards a major medical finding. He would keep appealing the verdict and stress how he was duped into accepting the terms of his plea bargain while they plotted to give him another thirty years for the second death. It just wasn't fair.

At *BIOFUTURE,* two lab techs were given the job of cleaning out Skip Chandler's desk, bench top area and his work in the incubator room and vivarium. In the tissue culture room, one noticed under the hood, three flasks of cells given codes that were not in the register of the lab chief, Dr. Simmons. She decided to look at the cells growing so silently. There sitting in the flasks on the stage of the inverted microscope, were many neurons connected and reaching out to their adjacent neighbors. She had never seen this intensity before. This was unusual. The second and third flasks were filled with the same kinds of connecting cells. The second tech returned from the vivarium and said that she had seen cages with Chandler's name on them. She didn't know that he had done animal surgeries. There were no records of the animals being operated on but it was clear that they had received some kind of surgery on their spinal cords. The scars were as plain as could be. The funny thing was they were running all around their cages. Dr. Simmons was leaving the company and didn't want to deal with the leftovers of "the unstable young man." The animals would have to go.

June Wilson, the younger of the two techs, felt a twinge of sadness when she held up the flasks of cells. Here was the life's work of a man she had long thought to be a genius. She had fantasized about a relationship with him but had never found the nerve to actually introduce herself to him. Perhaps now she had her chance to change all that. She wondered if he would probably welcome her attention. She took the cells and decided to freeze them and contact Skip in his new "residence." She would offer to help him continue his work by proxy. It would take a little finagling to work it all out but she was sure she could and would do it. The animals would be another story. She could rely on one of the men in the vivarium to set them aside temporarily. She would need to contact Skip about that sooner rather than later. Yes, she now had a most interesting purpose to drive her. She could finally show Skip that she was worthy.

Printed in the United States
By Bookmasters